Unfinished Business

"Mia Kerick has written a wonderful story of true love, haunting danger and trying to protect those you love, while adding in finding confidence in yourself and trusting those you love."

—MM Good Book Reviews

"The sex is intense and adds to the storyline."

—Gay List Book Reviews

"Unfinished Business is sure to stay with the reader long after they have finished the book."

—Top 2 Bottom Reviews

A Package Deal

"The book is an exceptionally good read. It's not a 'feel good' romp, but instead it's a masterful piece of writing that allows great character sketches to tell some very human stories which allow the reader to begin to love the characters and truly trust that everything happens for a reason because we are all destined to be happy in the end."

—MM Good Book Reviews

"This book is not a steamy, sexy romp, it isn't a quick and easy ride to a HEA, but it is a wonderful story and I highly recommend it."

—The Novel Approach

OUT OF HIDING

MIA KERICK

Dreamspinner Press

Published by
Dreamspinner Press
5032 Capital Circle SW
Suite 2, PMB# 279
Tallahassee, FL 32305-7886
USA
http://www.dreamspinnerpress.com/

ISBN: 978-1-62798-649-6
Digital ISBN: 978-1-62798-650-2

Printed in the United States of America
First Edition
January 2014

For Dreamspinner Press and Harmony Ink Press,
who have changed my life.

1

1

THE STAIRWAY in the old building had been hot, but the dance studio was nice and cool.

Too bad Dario Pereira wasn't.

When we got there, he was already inside the studio, fiddling around with his iPod, his back to the doorway. He didn't turn to greet us, although I was 99 percent certain he'd heard us come in.

"You're late." Even from behind, I couldn't miss the way Dario's head turned dramatically to the side as he raised his arm to take an overly long look at his shiny wristwatch. Come to think of it, outside on the sidewalk a couple of minutes ago, Sophie had inspected her own watch in exactly the same way, as she'd been stressing out about being late for her lesson with the crowned prince of dance. There was a round white clock with big black numbers mounted to the wall right in front of his nose, but he preferred to make the statement through his grandiose action. Call me perceptive, but I got his meaning easily, despite the fact that all I could see of him was his back side: short jet black hair cropped close to his skin at his neck and maybe some kind of swooping tuft-thing on the top, skin-tight black leggings on a fantastic butt (I'm shy, not blind), and a tight white T-shirt filled to the brim with compact dancer's muscles. Not bad at all.

"I'm sorry."

I looked over at Sophie; her cheeks now glowed brightly enough that you could hang them on the bow of a fishing boat at night and be confident you'd be seen by the other watercraft in the area. She didn't explain herself any further. Just the apology.

"I am certain it will not happen again." He waited a couple of seconds to let his meaning sink into our brains, which it did, quite effectively, and then he turned around. And *holy crap!* Dario Pereira's front side was even more impressive than his back side.

IN HER defense, Sophie had an excellent reason for being late, and it had "Uncle Phil" written all over it.

The walk from Steps on Broadway, where Sophie had taken her ballet class, to Ripley Grier Studios on 72nd Street, where she would have her first private lesson, was short. But it was really hot outside, fry an egg on the sidewalk kind of hot, and what had us sweating even more than the heat was the humidity. So after forcing Sophie to go into a deli to buy herself a couple of drinks, I'd stopped again to pull my longish brown hair into a low ponytail to keep me cool on the rest of the trip. But after walking just one more block, that low ponytail had been stuck to my neck like spaghetti to a wall, so I'd stopped again to tie it up into a messy bun. And it had felt so good when the air finally moved against my neck, I'd probably taken a minute or two to savor the feeling before getting moving again.

I'd surely been a sight: a heavily bearded dude sweating his butt off, a tiny sloppy bun perched precariously on the very top of his head, wearing a baggy dark-green Treehugger T-shirt complete with armpit stains and patchwork hemp cargo shorts that needed to be washed because I'd been wearing them for the past two days. And to complete the look, I wore beat up L.L.Bean hiking boots that still smelled of fish with the thick, knee-high wool socks that Henri had given me for Christmas last year poking up from underneath. And I couldn't neglect to mention my mandatory black JanSport backpack that was pretty much always strapped on my back. I carried that thing everywhere like a security blanket, even when it was empty; it had seen me through a lot. In any case, I don't think there's a label for my bedraggled kind of style, and remembering that, right there on the dark city street, a huge wave of self-consciousness had washed over me. I'd suddenly been overwhelmed by the inner knowledge that I didn't fit in this brightly lit, sophisticated city.

But when I'd stopped *one more time* to yank my red bandana out of my leg pocket, and I'd raised up my head to wipe off my sweaty face and neck, I'd sneaked a sideways glance at all the city-dwellers and tourists swarming past me. Nobody had been looking at me suspiciously, as if they were wondering, "What is that no-good hippy up to?" like they often did in the upscale, suburban North Shore of Massachusetts where I'd been raised. In fact, nobody had been looking at me *at all*, period, except for Sophie, who'd been busy glaring from me to her wristwatch and then back to me again, because she hadn't wanted to be late for her first private lesson with Dario Pereira.

It had taken me another long minute to fully digest that fact. In this oversized, chaotic city, nobody gave even a single crap, not to be crude, about Philippe Bergeron—not about the quantity of hair that was growing out of his face and head, what he was wearing, what he was up to, or where he was going. To them, Philippe Bergeron's scruffy face was just another one in the crowd. These people all had places to go, and my hairy mug, clearly, hadn't been one of the faces they were dashing off, in such a purposeful rush, to see.

And I'd felt small… like an inconsequential part of the scenery. Not like a target… and not in any way obvious. Just another dude on the street, lost in the crowd. I liked that feeling a lot.

"Uh, *hello*, Uncle Phil! Time to get your rear in gear." I remembered how she'd rolled her eyes with impatience.

"I'm coming, I'm coming, Sophie…. Give the old man a chance to mop up." I'd stuck my damp bandana into my back pocket, hooked my thumbs into my JanSport pack's straps, and we'd gotten back on our way.

So AS I was saying, Dario Pereira's front side was nothing short of amazing. His eyes were about as dark as the night sky over the Atlantic, and they lifted up slightly at the corners, but I didn't think he was Asian. Come to think of it, his eyes were hard to describe in words other than "suitable to write poems about," and even though I'm not one to write poems, I'm also not one to exaggerate. Beneath those captivating eyes, he had the most even facial features I think I'd ever seen, apart from the faces on the painted Native American dolls in Sophie's multicultural doll collection. All of these perfect features were set in creamy, coffee-colored skin. I'm not lying when I say that his skin was smooth enough to make even an introvert like me want to reach out and touch it.

And then he smiled. *Holy crap times two!* Briefly flashing these two perfect rows of chalk-white teeth, he moved directly over to Sophie, who looked like she was hoping to evaporate into thin air.

"But no harm done, dear. I simply want you to get your money's worth out of our lesson time. I do *not* come cheap." He looked at me squarely for the first time, and I had to wonder if he was sending me some sort of a subliminal message. After all, Henri told me that Dario had already been paid in full for this summer's services with Sophie, so cheap or not cheap—it made no real difference to me.

"Um, Sophie was at ballet class. We seriously busted our behinds to get over here as fast as we could, but, see, I made her stop and buy some drinks, because of the heat, and I didn't want her to keel over from the...." I allowed my voice to trail off, as it didn't really matter. We wouldn't be late again.

I felt the scourge of Dario's eyes as he scrutinized my perspiring body, my baggy clothing... my entire person. My shoulders lifted practically to my ears, like I was trying to crawl into myself, and I started shifting my weight from one foot to the other. *Cool as a cucumber, that's me.*

"Yes, I'm sure." And just like that, he looked away from me—I'd been dismissed. He never even changed that haughty expression, which didn't so much anger me as make me feel that I was nothing but a piece of you-know-what in Dario's perfect eyes. Come to think of it, other than that brief smile, he hadn't made any facial expressions at all since we'd arrived at the studio. "Sophie, please go to the mirror and neaten your bun a bit. Loose wisps of hair in your face will only distract us both. And then please remove your outdoor clothing. I want you to be wearing just a leotard—I prefer black—and tights. Pink or black only. Transition tights from now on, please, as I will need to see your feet."

At this point, we were both gawking at him out of a combination of awe at his beauty, fear at his intensity, and shame for daring to make him wait five minutes for us. Sophie recovered from her shock before I did and scrambled over to the mirror, where she was frantically pushing pins into her hair.

Again, Dario turned to me, and this time I could put a label on the expression he wore, or, at least, I thought I could. (In all honesty, though, sometimes I have a tendency toward paranoia.) I was almost certain that his face betrayed disgust, but just a tiny trace of it. Dario seemed to possess the self-control of Mahatma Gandhi, and if he wanted to refrain from appearing disgusted, all he had to do was look bored.

"We do not wear outdoor shoes in the studio, sir. Please remove your… um, *boots*… and place them by the doorway."

I looked at him sideways, unaccustomed to being handled quite so efficiently. I mean, I was a tall guy, and bearded… and kind of gruff. I'd actually grown the beard to make people back off. (And to cover the boyishness, that I was pretty sure still lingered so plainly beneath it—but nobody else needed to know that.) Before I even had a chance to scowl, though, Dario had removed his attention from me completely, and for the next hour and a half, he put Sophie through what amounted to physical torture. *They* called it "floor barre."

Sophie never got up off the floor once.

I sat cross-legged in the corner, my itchy wool socks rubbing against the Marley floor, watching and listening to the entire lesson. And even though I was intimidated by his abrasiveness, I admitted that Dario was nothing if not mesmerizing, in both his beauty and his gracefulness. As they worked, both of their brows were furrowed and their lips tightened into matching straight lines. They were so deep in concentration on this passion that made them whole, and I experienced a momentary panic that I would never find something to occupy my head and my heart that way. And I was certain I wouldn't ever fit in any place the way Dario and Sophie fit inside this dance studio. I shook my shaggy head a few times to banish the thought.

For a few moments, I allowed my mind to wander. The two dancers working so diligently in front of me had no real need of my opinion, my lacking sense of humor, or even my presence, but still, here I was, so I found myself revisiting the day of our arrival in the big city.

ONE MORE time, how did I end up here? I'd asked myself yet again as I'd stood there, my feet basically glued to the sidewalk. The teenage girl who'd hovered in my shadow apparently shared my bewilderment, because she'd squeezed my hand and said, "Well, we're here, *Uncle Phil*." Sophie only played the "Uncle Phil" card when she was feeling, in some way, out of sorts. She had then looked up at me with a "now what?" expression that I could totally relate to.

"Looks like we made it, Soph." Realizing too late that my words sounded like a cheesy song from the 1980s, I'd turned my attention toward the cab driver. He'd already dropped our bags on the street and was gawking at me expectantly as I stood there in a bit of a daze, holding hands with my niece. And he just so happened to be wearing that same "now what?" expression I'd just seen on Sophie's face, which had served to rouse me from my stupor. "Oh… oh, yeah… you must want money."

The driver, well, he hadn't smiled or nodded or anything. He'd just kept on staring at me, all stone-faced, until I'd reached into my back pocket and pulled out my wallet. I'd paid the guy, tipped him well with my big brother's money, and then I'd stopped short and thought about it. (Decisiveness, I'm afraid, has never been one of my defining qualities.)

"What the he…." I allowed my voice to trail off because I always tried very hard not to curse. Then I opened my wallet again and threw the dude another ten. Henri could afford it.

In a nutshell, that's just about *exactly* how the two of us ended up here, in New York City, for the better part of the summer.

By my much older stepbrother Henri Bergeron's direct command, which he liked to call a "request."

"YOU CAN hold that up there longer; I saw you do it before. Just use the muscle in the back of your thigh."

Seeing as Dario was still standing over Sophie, cracking his figurative whip so she'd perform her very best, there was no reason I couldn't continue to daydream. So I let my consciousness travel back to, if not better days, easier-for-me-to-handle ones. And inside of a mere minute, I was drifting on the Atlantic. The ocean was never far from my mind. Way out there on the water, past those last lonely glimpses of land—the ones that jut up out of the ocean like a serpent's bumpy back—had been the only place I'd even come close to fitting in. I'd especially liked it out there at night, and I could remember just how it felt. With my feet planted on the boat's spotless deck (I'd swabbed it with my own two hands) and wobbling around like it was my first time on a skateboard, I'd savored the freedom that had come from being hidden by a black blanket of night. I couldn't see my hand, even when I'd held it a couple of inches in front of my nose, because it'd just been so blindingly dark out there.

Unless, of course, it had been one of those starry nights, the ones when the sky was scattered with millions upon millions of tiny dots of light. Those had been the nights when I'd felt *really* small… insignificant, even. Not that feeling small had ever been a problem for me because honestly it had always been the opposite. Feeling as minute as one single star in an infinite night sky had helped me feel lost, the thing I'd always wanted most.

Being lost…. I smiled as I delighted in the sound of those two sweet words. Being lost, completely buried in the chaos of life, had long been my truest goal. Because when I was "lost" out there on the ocean, I'd fit in. And I'd fit in because I'd *almost* disappeared.

"ONE MORE time, Sophie. I know you are tired, but I want you to show me that you have the strength in you to do the exercise just *one more time*…." My niece had turned an alarming shade of red, and was panting.

And seeing her panic, my mind was dragged away again, back to my initial panic at first encountering my temporary home, New York City. I wasn't going to say that I didn't feel small in these new surroundings because, God knew, I did. In fact, every time I looked up and saw a cluster of tall, gray skyscrapers, towering over like they meant to crush me, or felt the rude nudge of an insistent crowd pushing in against me on all sides, those nasty honks and a buzz of languages I didn't know from Adam filling up my ears, I didn't feel small in the way I wanted. I felt small like a sparkling silver minnow splashing around aimlessly in the dark murky ocean—targeted and obvious. But here in New York City, or Midtown Manhattan, if you liked to be exact, I couldn't afford to blend into the background. Because right here, right now, I had to be the responsible one: Mr. In-Charge.

"YOU MAY wonder why I'm having you do such an intense floor barre tonight, when you are here to learn a dance solo, Sophie. But before we can start working on a solo in a new style, I want to see where you are in terms of ballet technique, strength, and flexibility. And if we need to correct any of the basics, this is the best place for us to start. We have the entire summer to get you fully prepared for your college audition solo."

Sophie had said pretty close to nothing for the entire ninety minutes we were in that studio, but that fact didn't seem to faze Dario. He chattered on and on about how she needed to keep her back straight, and her hips square, and, please, not to force her turnout, whatever that was. He pushed his flat palms against her back, pressed his thumbs on her hip bones, and knelt right down on the floor to move her feet into the exact position he wanted them. By the end of the lesson, Sophie was beet red, panting, sweating, and, from what I could see, frustrated. But Dario didn't seem to have a clue as to her physical exhaustion or her potential emotional breakdown.

At the lesson's end, he stepped away from her, went to the corner where he had left his iPod, backpack, and water bottle, and then, after taking a few quick sips of water, he pulled jeans on over his black leggings and slid his pretty bare feet into Italian loafers.

"I will see you, Sophie, on Thursday, at five *sharp*." There was no "atta girl, Soph!" No "nice job, kid!" Dario Pereira just turned on his stylish heel and strutted right out of the room, calling, "Be sure to turn out the lights and close the door before you leave. This isn't a barn." He made this snorting sound and then was gone.

With great effort, Sophie dragged herself up off the floor, turned to look at me, and then burst into tears. And since I had no idea what to do with one hundred and ten pounds of crying female, I stepped forward, hugged her kind of impulsively, and said the only thing I could think of.

"Don't you think it's time for an ice cream cone?"

Between sobs, she managed to choke out, "F-fat f-free f-frozen y-yogurt...."

2

IN NEW York City, just to get from one place to another, we did more walking than we did back home in Massachusetts. At home, all you had to do was walk half the length of the driveway to get into the car, or maybe the full length to get the mail. And on these long walks through the NYC blocks, Sophie and I didn't exactly talk each other's ears off, but once in a while, she'd ask me an in-your-face question that led to brief conversation.

This morning we were going to visit the Fordham College dance program. We decided that we'd eat breakfast at a local diner once we got to Lincoln Center. Soph had her mind set on her breakfast being an egg-white omelet. I knew that because she'd told me three separate times.

"So how come we aren't staying in the Trump International Hotel and Tower or the Four Seasons Hotel, Phil? Those two hotels are way more my dad's speed."

"Believe me, he tried. When he proposed this 'summer in the city' plan, I straight out told him that I wasn't going to stay in any hotel where they'd eye me suspiciously every time I cross the lobby, like they were afraid I'd steal something."

"And he just said, 'okay, fine'? That doesn't sound much like the father I know."

"I told him enough is enough—no five-star hotels. And I think he knew if he pushed me too hard I'd go sprinting back to the ocean."

Sophie nodded, getting the picture. "That's the last thing he wants. He's always so scared that you won't come back from a fishing trip."

I chose to ignore that remark. My job on the fishing boat had been a major bone of contention in the Bergeron household. "I feel bad that he's paying for all this, you know, with my 'brand-new-big-brother-financed platinum credit card.' Plus, he insisted on getting us adjoining rooms—we could've just stayed together in one—and then there's food and travel and—"

"And all of my dance classes... but you know that money is not an issue for him. And this is your *job* this summer. You're getting paid to put up with me."

"I guess Henri figured that since I have the time and need the work, I could do this for him. You *know* that his business won't let him get away, right?"

She nodded. "I'm not the one who's having trouble with Dad doling out the cash."

"And you're okay with the step down in accommodations?"

"The Holiday Inn is fine, Phil."

Better than anywhere I'd crashed when I was fishing in Gloucester, that's for sure. "Yeah, it's safe, and clean... and it has a pool."

"And it actually has room service." I looked over at Sophie and saw a red mark on her shoulder from where her dance bag strap was cutting into her skin. I snatched it from her hand and threw it over my own aching shoulder. Chivalry was not dead when it came to my niece, who was actually much more like a little sister... but feeling the weight of the bag on my shoulder, I thought that she sure carried around way too much crap.

When we'd arrived in NYC, Sophie had two humongous rolling suitcases. I, on the other hand, not being deeply invested in material possessions, had one medium-sized duffel bag. And to be honest, what I'd packed in that bag could have gotten me through an entire year, let alone a short summer. The rest of my earthly possessions were packed in two boxes that had been stuck in the corner of a guest bedroom at Henri's minimansion in Essex, Massachusetts. God knew the man had plenty of room there, especially since Sophie's mother, Louisa, and her little brother, Stefan, had been killed in a car accident when Sophie was in middle school.

Don't go there, Philippe.

It was time for a mental subject change. "Hey, here's a diner.... We have plenty of time to get breakfast before the tour." I looked her up and down, intending to be obvious about it. Sophie was tall and on the slim side with light hair and skin. She looked like she could use a good meal (or two). "I'm starving—could eat a horse. But don't get one of tasteless egg-white thingies, all right? You need some *real* food."

We went into the crowded diner and found seats across from each other, in the far corner. In her very Sophie-like way, she jabbed the menu into my face, and I had to whisk it away from her, almost defensively, to prevent her from poking my eye out with the thing. "I *like* egg-white omelets, *Uncle Phil.* And, besides, nobody wants a fat ballerina."

So she'd started referring to me as "Uncle Phil" again. In other words, Sophie was perturbed. "I thought that we were here to look at *modern* dance programs, Soph. And we watched plenty of videos of modern dance companies at your house before we left, right? From what I remember, modern dancers can have much more meat on their bones than ballet dancers, so you won't have to spend your entire life obsessed with what food you *can't* eat."

Sophie had never been exactly anorexic, but lately, Henri had told me that he'd become concerned that she'd grown overly obsessed with her body image, probably thanks to years of spending six nights a week in those mirrored ballet studios surrounded by a bunch of girls obsessed with starving themselves until they had "ballet bodies." And since Sophie wanted nothing other than to be a professional dancer, the bribe from Henri went like this: I will support you in attending a college with a modern dance program where you can get a Bachelor of Fine Arts degree in performance, or even in a professional modern dance training program, but I will not support you in becoming an apprentice at a ballet company at almost eighteen years old. For once in a blue moon, I'd agreed with my brother. From what I could see, the ballet world was harsh.

But what part of the world isn't harsh?

And then there was me. Not that I was in any way qualified for the job, but I was Sophie's chaperone.

Maybe she could tell I was getting lost in thought, which was not at all unusual for me, because she looked at me brazenly, a subtle challenge in her eyes, and she informed me, "Nobody wants a fat modern dancer, either."

"Don't you dare try to speak for everybody, young lady." I used my haughtiest I'm-the-adult-here voice, which was a major stretch for me. (I sometimes thought bossy thoughts, but I never could manage to make them come out of my mouth the way they sounded in my head.) "I, for one, think you would look adorable with a cute little roll around your gut."

"You're gay, Phil, what do you know about how a girl should look?" When Sophie said stuff like that, she wasn't being rude, just a little bit snarky, but that was okay in my book. Sophie needed to show the world that she had a backbone, so why not start with her reclusive "Uncle Phil"?

I rolled my eyes, because if I made a major effort, I could be *slightly* snarky too, and then scratched at my chin through my shaggy beard. "How about a bacon, egg, and cheese biscuit... or two?"

Shaking her head, she snatched the menu out of my hands and opened it with some heavy teenage-girl attitude, which was similar to what I remembered from the girls I was in high school with a few years ago. And then she grimaced. "*Perfect...* no egg-white omelets on the menu," she mumbled. "This is *so* not turning out to be my day. All they have is *regular omelets* in this nasty dive. Are you satisfied, *Uncle Phil*?"

"Perfectly."

A FEW hours later, we'd finished our tour of the Fordham College Lincoln Center campus, and more importantly, to Sophie, at least, we were now headed over to take a tour of the nearby Alvin Ailey American Dance Theater. The Fordham College student tour guide, who'd seemed confused about which one of us was applying to the school, had said this was the place where the Fordham BFA students took all their dance classes.

The Joan Weill Center that housed the Alvin Ailey School was an amazing sight, inside and out: ultramodern, lots of windows and roomy studios, all in top-notch condition. When I entered, I could sense a palpable feeling of pride. At breakfast, Sophie had informed me that Alvin Ailey was an African-American choreographer who had been credited with making modern dance more popular with the American public. She'd also told me that Ailey was a social activist, responsible for first including African Americans in concert dance in the United States. So it seemed that the man who gave this dance program its name had the deepest roots in modern dance. I supposed this was as good a place as any to start our exploration.

Now, I didn't know the first thing about ballet technique, but Sophie did. So the first thing we did after the tour, was spend some time checking out a ballet class.

We sat down in a couple of folding metal chairs that had been placed at an angle for visitor seating on the far side of the room.

"Most modern dance programs require students to take ballet class every day," Sophie whispered to me. Class hadn't started yet, so I had no idea why she was whispering, but I still nodded and kept my lips zipped. The dancers were all noticeably focused—there was no chitchat going on among them at all—or even any smiles that I could see.

We watched them work at the barre for more than thirty minutes. What surprised me most was that the teacher approached the students and touched them, adjusting the positions of their arms and legs, pressing on backs, and tapping on hips to adjust the dancers' postures, what appeared to be no more than a quarter of an inch in one direction or another. I'd always thought it was an unspoken rule that teachers keep their hands off their students, but apparently, that rule didn't apply in ballet class. I leaned over to ask Sophie about this, but she refused to acknowledge my attempt to talk to her. Well, other than the scathing "shut up, Uncle Phil" look she sent me.

To Sophie's credit, there *did* seem to be a strict no-talking rule in ballet. The environment in the studio was formal and proper, right down to the curtseys and bows offered to the teacher at the end of class, which was a rather unexpected sight for me. But Henri had told me that when it came to ballet, Sophie was one tough customer, and she seemed to like what she saw, so it was all good.

WHAT STRUCK me harder than ballet, though, was the Horton modern dance class we got to observe. A traditional style of modern that had been inspired by American Indian tribal dances (I'm not just spouting nonsense, I'd actually *paid attention* during the building tour), Horton had also been a major part of Alvin Ailey's dance training. In this class, the students, who were still entirely professional, maybe even fierce-looking with their solid black attire and their slicked-back, neatly pinned hair, gave off a new sense of freedom as they made shapes with their bodies. Flat backs, deep squats, and sideways stretches. And, I've got to admit, what everybody said about dancers was true: they were *very* flexible.

As the class went on, most of the dancers got really into it, and the pounding beats of the live drummer set up in the corner didn't diminish the primitive atmosphere. In time to the music, the dancers swung their legs, lunged down low, and at the end of class, propelled their bodies across the floor, using turns and jumps with a sort of "wild abandon" that I'd never seen in any of Sophie's ballet recitals. And I'd attended as many of those recitals as I could, up until I'd headed east to fish.

Sophie was wide-eyed as she watched the Horton Modern class. I couldn't really tell if she liked it. She didn't say anything at all to me, and, believe me, I didn't lean over to ask her any more questions. Beside the fact that I knew she'd cut out my tongue if I tried to speak again during class, Sophie and I weren't the sort of people who needed to speak just for the sake of making noise. So the persistent silence between us, all by itself, wasn't unusual.

As we walked along the sidewalk toward the subway (I'd insisted that we use public transportation like *regular* people when we were going somewhere together, instead of cabs and limos, which would have been Henri's choice), Sophie stopped for a minute, looked up at me, her blue eyes squinted thoughtfully, and announced, "I like the location of Fordham's Lincoln Center campus, and I think Dad would like the quality of the education here. The ballet is good, but... can we come back to the Ailey studios later this week? I think I'd like to try some of the open adult Horton classes they offer. And I think they also offer Horton at Steps on Broadway."

For Sophie, that was nothing short of a dissertation, and I hoped I wasn't staring at her, my shock at her loose lips evident. "Sure. When we get back to the hotel, let's look online at Ailey's adult class schedules... and we can check out Steps on Broadway's too."

She nodded, started walking again, and without turning back, informed me, "And Phil, remember that tonight I have a private lesson with Dario. We're meeting him at Ripley-Grier Studios on 72nd at ten, after I take a ballet class at Steps on Broadway."

"Ten? Isn't that kind of late for you? I mean... to *start* a lesson?"

Sophie gave me one of those put-upon teenager looks, ones that I was probably sending adults not too long ago. I've actually got to take that back; even at twenty, I was still in the habit of shooting that "you've got to be kidding me" expression at any older adult who annoyed me. "Oh… oh, yeah. That's right, so ten o'clock, it is."

"And I expect you to put a little more spring in your step on our walk over to my lesson; I'm not gonna let *you* make me late again." And just like that Sophie was finished with our little chat. She pulled her subway pass out of her dance bag, slid it across the card slot, and pushed through the gate, leaving me to trail along behind her.

3

I MISSED the water. And I didn't mean just in the sense of missing the wide-open ocean and the nighttime sky, and that sense of being small; I actually missed the feeling of being submerged in water. Growing up near the ocean, swimming for relaxation and exercise had been an activity I'd grown to enjoy. *The freedom... and the weightlessness.* So I'll start with the good news: the Holiday Inn had a rooftop pool. The bad news: it was already eighty-five degrees and humid and it was only ten in the morning. I had a sneaking suspicion that I wouldn't be alone in that rooftop pool today. But since I had safely delivered Sophie to Peridance Capezio Center, where she was going to take three classes in a row—a Pilates, a ballet, and a beginner modern—which added up to four and a half hours, I decided I wouldn't hole up in a crowded dance school waiting area. I figured, why not wait in a crowded pool instead?

When I stepped out on the rooftop pool deck, the very first thing that went through my mind was, "I won't be swimming laps here." Scattered like pebbles all throughout the pool, were toddlers attached to their parents, bigger kids splashing around wildly, shouting, "Marco!" or "Polo!", and old ladies perched on the pool's edges, doing kicking exercises. But all of these people were there to feel free and weightless, just like I was, so I was okay with the crowd. I dropped my backpack onto a green-cushioned lounge chair that I could see from the water, stepped to the pool's edge, and slithered right in.

The water was warm. *Maybe it's a bit too warm*, I thought, as I took a look at all of the swim diapers on the babies and toddlers. But since I'd never been a germaphobe, I dunked my head under, shook the hair off my face when my head popped up, and started to tread water.

No. It definitely wasn't the Atlantic Ocean, but still, it was refreshing. And although I wasn't one to chat up the guy beside me, I did get a kick out of people-watching, so as I paddled my way through the water, I observed the "hot babes" dousing themselves with baby oil, the young fathers dragging their kids back and forth through the water, probably wishing they had cold beers in their hands instead, and the moms…. To be honest, I tried not to look at the mothers too closely. I again admitted to myself that I still hadn't fully recovered from losing my own mom when I was in fifth grade.

Probably I'll never get over it.

But if one positive thing came of losing Mom to cancer when I was a kid, it was that I was able to really *be there* for Sophie when she'd lost her own mother and brother just over four years ago, because I'd truly *been there* in every sense, and Sophie knew it. Thanks to unfortunate coincidence, both of us had been in grade school—I'd been in fifth grade and Sophie in eighth—when our lives had fallen apart at the seams in very much the same way, except that she'd also lost her little brother, whereas I'd *been* the little brother. We'd also both been introverts, even before our mothers' deaths, and we'd been completely overwhelmed by the boatload of attention and sympathy showered on us by people who were trying their best to help us feel better. To put it bluntly, both of us had almost drowned in pools of loving kindness. All we could do if we wanted to breathe was to run and hide. Sophie hid in dance class; I was still trying to figure out where to hide.

One little blond-haired boy kept on swimming over toward me and was continually being summoned by his mom who sat in a chair she'd dragged to the edge of pool. But the lady had a phone tucked pretty much permanently under her chin and looked like her mind was about a million miles away from her son and the crowded pool; the last thing she must've wanted was to have her precious angel hanging around with a long-haired, bearded, biker-looking dude like me. This last time, though, the determined little boy made it all the way to my side.

"I can swim all by myself." Visibly proud, he looked up at me with eyes of dark brown, the challenge in them reminding me a little bit of Dario.

I smiled. "I can see that."

"Didn't even take swimming lessons, mister. My daddy showed me how to do it at the ocean… but Daddy's mostly gone now." His arms and legs were motoring about a mile a minute, and he was still looking up at me with a crooked, squinting grin. "My name is Tommy."

I glanced over at his mother, who was fully involved in her phone conversation. "Hi, Tommy. I'm Philippe."

"Hi, Flip."

That was darn cute, so I let it go.

"I'm four."

That's a young age to swim, isn't it? I was curious.

Then he looked at me expectantly, like he was waiting for me to report my own age to him, but instead I said, "You're a very big boy."

He nodded, satisfied with my reply. Just then his mother glanced up. Truly, the lady didn't look like a mom who belonged poolside. She was wearing a tan business suit that was sprinkled with dots of pool water, her light brown hair was pulled back into a tight bun, like the ballerinas wore, and she clutched an iPhone and an iPad.

"Oh, Tommy! Leave the poor man alone!" She stood up, kicked off her pumps, and stepped over to the edge of the pool near the place we were swimming. "I'm so sorry, sir. Tommy is just very lonely, and he knows how to find a friendly face in a crowd."

Me? A friendly face? Is she for real?

"Come on, Tommy. Let the man swim in peace."

My lips were talking before my brain had engaged. "He's fine here, ma'am. If it's okay with you, he can swim with me."

"Really? I don't want to put you out." She looked relieved.

"No, it's fine. My name is Philippe, and I guess I'm sort of a nanny, or a 'manny,' maybe, this summer… for my seventeen-year-old niece. I like kids of all ages."

"Oh my God, thank you, Philippe. I have a couple of phone calls to make, and they're very important, like life or death important, you know? I'll be right over there at that table. Thank you so much."

During his mom's phone call, Tommy showed me his kid's version of the freestyle and the backstroke. I gave him a couple of pointers, and he picked up on them quickly.

"Good work, Tommy. You sure you're not part dolphin?"

Tommy laughed out loud and then squeaked like a dolphin a few times. "Will you throw me, Flip? Into the water—like that daddy over there is doing to his girl?"

And so I did. He swam to me, and I lifted him by his gangly arms and tossed him about two feet. Tommy sank under the water, emerged already grinning, and shrieked, "Again!"

After about five minutes of doing this over and over, I could tell that the little dude was getting tired. "How about a piggyback ride?"

Little Tommy latched right on to my shoulders, snug as my JanSport backpack, and I gave him a complete seahorse tour of the pool, dipping down under the surface of the water every now and then to keep things interesting.

"Philippe... Philippe...." All of a sudden, it seemed, Tommy's mother was standing by the edge of the pool again. I realized I'd gotten rather caught up in playing with Tommy. "I don't know how to thank you.... I'm finished with my phone calls, my divorce lawyer, among other things."

"Sorry to hear that. And don't worry, it wasn't a problem at all, ma'am."

"It's Lauren. Lauren Davis." I lifted Tommy up out of the pool and into her waiting arms, and then she wrapped him up in a colorful beach towel.

"I don't normally pawn Tommy off on total strangers, but my husband and I are divorcing, as I said, and I'm moving to the city, with Tommy, of course, and right now, I'm trying to find a place to live. I really needed a few minutes to make calls, so I could set up some appointments to look at apartments."

"Uh... Lauren, like I said, it was no problem. We had fun." *We really had.*

"Flip is my best friend."

Although it was bright up there on the rooftop, I could sure see that Lauren was blushing. "Tommy, honey, Philippe is a grown man. We'll go to the park and find you some friends your own age after we look at a couple of new homes, okay?"

"Okay, Mommy. But Flip is still my best friend."

Lauren started to protest, but I let her off the hook. "We *are* pretty tight, Lauren."

She grinned at me, and it was a crooked grin, like Tommy's. "You are one of a kind, Philippe."

Then she took Tommy by the hand, turned and grabbed her bag, and then led him to the exit. Tommy glanced back at me a couple of times, not with worry, but with a child's naïve confidence that he'd just made a new best friend; the fact that I was twenty years old and a hippy-fisherman while he was an adorable four-year-old boy didn't even factor in. I waved. And I felt good. Better than "lost in the stars" good.

Almost.

4

WE WERE on our way to check out classes at the Martha Graham School of Contemporary Dance. Midmorning, we planned to watch an advanced Graham technique class at the Westbeth Artists Housing building in the West Village, and later in the day, we'd observe a ballet class in The Graham Foundation's other location on 63rd Street.

The Westbeth building provided affordable living and working space for artists in NYC, and the free-spirited hippy in me was like, "Super cool, man!" It was also the home of the Martha Graham Dance Foundation, where the company's advanced classes were offered. The building was surely an older one and quirky in its artistic spirit. It had its own gallery and the community room that got used for all different kinds of performance, as well as for dance classes and rehearsal spaces.

As we stepped off the elevator into the Martha Graham dance space, Sophie slipped into introvert mode, which wasn't surprising. We weren't going on an official tour this time. Instead, we were there to see an advanced class, which would show us the direction Sophie would be heading if she decided to get her training there.

In our usual total silence, we sat in the lobby and waited for class to get underway. The dancers who came in looked much older and more sophisticated than Sophie. And as each dancer entered, I noticed Sophie shrink down a bit more into her chair.

"Don't try to talk to me during class, *Uncle* Phil. It's embarrassing."

"Don't worry. I learned my lesson on that at Alvin Ailey."

She looked suitably chastised and offered me a small smile. "It's nothing personal."

But she didn't need to explain herself to me because I understood. She wanted to blend into the background in life almost as much as I did. In fact, the only time she wanted to stand out was when she was on a stage and her movement was fully choreographed.

"I get it, Soph."

"If I was to go here for dance training, I'd have to study my academic subjects at a nearby college or at an online university so I could get my degree. Dad is insisting that I get 'educated,' whether I like it or not."

"Yeah. Your dad wants us to check out City College of New York, if you end up liking it here."

And even though she wasn't going to take class, Sophie got down on the floor to stretch. I guess it was just her habit, or, more probably, part of her effort to blend into the background.

"What do you know about Martha Graham?" I hoped I could get her to loosen up a little with conversation, but at the same time, I knew it could just as easily backfire and I'd be left talking to myself.

From her place on the floor, Sophie looked up at me and answered simply, "Many people say that she is the mother of modern dance."

"What does that mean, exactly?"

Sophie looked around to make sure no one was close enough to overhear her interpretations of the woman who this whole foundation was named after. "Martha Graham brought dance into the twentieth century by introducing serious societal issues to the stage. Like the Wall Street Crash… and the Great Depression and…. Well, she brought the emotions of depression and isolation, you know, *dark things*, to public awareness."

I was surprised by the depth of her knowledge on the topic, but more so by her eloquence.

"Many people say that she created Modern Dance. The Graham technique has rules and exercises, just like ballet does. I've heard it takes ten years to fully master."

"How do you know all of this?"

She smiled and then glanced away from me shyly. "I read Martha Graham's biography. I chose it last semester for the basis of my Women in American History project. Graham was truly a feminist in how she dealt with women's issues on stage and in that she dared to move her body in such a way that they considered it to be totally radical back then. She just focused her choreography and her performance on emotion and… and on each emotion that people feel."

Every once in a while, this niece of mine managed to pull the rug out from under my feet. "You've sure done your homework on Martha Graham, kid." I liked to tease her by calling her "kid" every once in a while, because, although she was my niece, she was very close to my own age due to the fact that my father had married my mother late in life, and surprise, along came me when he already had a twenty-year-old son.

"Come on, *Uncle* Phil. It's time to go in." Sophie had no problem giving it right back to me. She got up, and I followed her into the spacious, high-ceilinged studio, over to some chairs that had been set up for observers. We sat down, and I prepared myself for an hour and a half of staring at strangers as they moved to music.

But Sophie tugged on my T-shirt sleeve. "Look… Dario's here."

I felt my head jolt up without my brain's permission, and my eyes started scanning the crowd of about eighteen dancers. Then I saw him, and he was every bit as beautiful as I remembered. But Dario was so focused on stretching that he didn't notice we were there, which was fine by me, seeing as I already knew that I was going to have to try very hard not to stare at him.

Just then, a male teacher came in, and the students stood and greeted him politely, then the room became silent. From the moment the drumbeats started and they began their floor exercises, all of the dancers' faces became still and serious, their eyes all focused straight ahead. The only way I could describe how they began their movement was that it reminded me of how a baby starts out in life. From their full bodies lying on the floor like helpless infants, they gradually moved on to sitting and then to kneeling. As they "grew up" from babies to toddlers, they did exercises that seemed to require every ounce of their concentration. The dancers breathed in a fierce manner for a time and soon began these majestic spiraling movements that started with their bellies and ended with their heads. A couple of times, they made figure eights with their whole bodies, releasing and contracting their middles, rising and falling in time to the drumbeats.

Again, I found Dario to be mesmerizing. Not only was his movement captivating, but also I could hardly keep myself from staring at the definition of his sleek muscles. From head to toe, he was the very image of the statues I'd seen when I'd visited the Museum of Fine Arts in Boston with Henri and Sophie last year. And to see Dario writhing around on the floor, swinging his legs, pointing and flexing and stretching and…. well, there weren't polite words for how it made me feel, so I'd have to leave it at that. I could say that I wanted to get down on the floor and do these movements right beside him, as in, very close to his side, maybe even touching him. The other night he'd been Dario, the teacher—correcting, pushing, proper—but right then, he was Dario, the artist. His body's movement was the work of art he was trying to control without restraining, to allow to flow without collapsing.

More fascinating even than the way his body was able to seem both fragile and strong at the very same time, was the expression of passion he wore. I was stunned by the commitment I saw on his face. And in a sudden whoosh, I understood a true fact about Dario, and about Sophie, as well. Dancing was not a hobby for these two people, and it would never be merely a job. Dancing was a need that had to be met.

After class, the students applauded the teacher, as well as the drummer in the corner of the room. I had to admit, I'd hardly been aware of the talented drummer thanks to Dario's captivating movement. One by one, the students spoke to the teacher before leaving the room, and after Dario left, never having even noticed us, Sophie thanked the teacher politely for letting us observe. By the time we left the studio, Dario was gone. But I wouldn't forget what I'd seen him do that day.

After we left the Westbeth building, I took Sophie out to lunch at one of the many eclectic cafés in the West Village. She hadn't yet uttered a single word about what we'd seen in the Graham Modern class. I was fine with that, as I knew she needed time to digest what she'd observed, so she could absorb it into her brain and make sense of it.

"Your dad is expecting us to call sometime today… to fill him in on what we've been up to so far."

She looked up from her Greek salad and said to me plainly, "Well, you can tell him that we observed Advanced Graham Technique class and that you lusted after my private dance teacher for the full ninety minutes."

"It was that obvious?" I tried not to let my inner panic attack twist my face.

"Not to him… he was in 'the zone.' I don't think he even noticed us at all."

"But it was obvious to you?"

"I'll put it this way: I almost handed you a tissue so you could wipe the drool off your chin."

I lifted my lemonade and guzzled down the half glass that was left, as if that would help to cool down my burning cheeks. "I guess I need to be more... more, uh, aware of how I'm acting."

"If anyone is gonna be the teacher's pet, Uncle Phil, it had better be me." Sophie smiled, teasing me. "But he *is* hot."

"That he is."

We exchanged conspiratorial smiles and finished lunch in our usual silence.

5

WHITE-MASKED faces with living red eyes, all of them focused squarely on me, were everywhere I looked... and I mean everywhere. Must have passed a hundred as I came in from playing basketball in the driveway—those things were scattered all over our front lawn like a flock of Canadian geese. One was even perched on top of the mailbox. Inside, they hung on the wall in a huge diamond shape around the television in the family room, and one of them rested upright on each step of the stairs, so close to my feet that I nearly trampled them as I ran up to get to my room. The worst part was that they pretty much overtook my bedroom like they owned it.

Somehow I knew I wasn't allowed to touch them, so I couldn't rip them off where they'd stuck themselves on top of my posters of LeBron James and David Ortiz and Tom Brady, and then chuck them out the window; and I couldn't shove them from off the top of my dresser and stomp them into mangled little scraps of paper mâché once they hit the floor. Because that would mean I'd have to touch them, which would be so completely against the rules that I could barely even make myself think it.

I had no idea who had made up these rules, but in any event, I just knew that it wasn't my place to question them.

Inside my head, I could somehow hear what the brains behind the masks were thinking. "We can see you, Philippe... you are the only thing we see... you can't hide from us... we only want to help you, dear... look at us, Philippe, in our eyes... God helps those who help themselves... don't look away from us, it's rude... he's such a quiet boy... we think that maybe he's mentally unstable... Philippe, you need to eat more... you don't look very good today... just try to smile, young man... you are completely losing it... we can see you, Philippe...."

Those masks just never shut up.

If I wanted to get into bed and pull the covers over my head, I would have to do it by climbing in underneath my bedspread, because there were about twenty masks laid out in the shape of a big, creepy smiley face on top of my bed that I wasn't supposed to touch. So I lay down flat on my belly on the floor beside my bed, carefully avoiding the fifteen or so masks that rested on my shaggy royal blue rug, and I slid like a snake, up underneath the blankets and onto the mattress. Once I was lying flat on the bed on my belly, I flipped over onto my back and then I bent my knees; I could feel the weight of the masks on top of the bedspread slipping down the sides of my legs. And I knew that somehow, even as I lay hidden by the blankets, every single last one of those piercing red eyes in my room could still see me. Clear as day... like I was naked in the school auditorium, in front of the whole fifth grade.

My feelings—all of my hurt and my shame and my guilt—were all exposed to everybody.

There was nowhere for me to hide.

And that's when I saw her. She was humming; I could tell that she'd been expecting me.

I breathed in her scent... ahhh, flowers. I actually felt her presence, as she was barely even an arm's length away from me. Maybe she could hide me from all of those nosy, prying red eyes that wouldn't stop probing, examining, observing....

If anyone could stop those eyes, Mom could.

So I thrust my arm out and reached for her, managing to grasp the side of her arm! Giddy with relief, I pinched my fingers tight around her skin to grip her so that I could pull her in my direction, but when I squeezed, her arm just vanished. I held only powder in my palm.

No, not powder... but more, oily, black ashes.

I lifted my ash-covered hand to my nose; it smelled of death, not flowers.

I reached out again, nothing short of frantic, though, at the same time certain that if I could just catch her, she would make the eyes look away. But this time when I fisted my palm around hers, it flaked up like crumbs from a day-old pastry, which then got lifted up and scattered in the sudden breeze.

Soon my mom was gone, like she'd never been there at all.

And all that was left was me—well, me and those red staring eyes.

I SHOT up in my hotel bed. My sheets were soaking; *I* was soaking.

"Phil… you were making noises. Are you alright?" Sophie poked her head through the adjoining doorway between our rooms, which we always kept open, and peered in at me.

"Um… I… uh, I think I was dreaming, Soph. Sorry to wake you." Another one of those messed-up dreams. I had hoped I wouldn't have one while I was staying here with Sophie.

She walked over to my bed and sat down gingerly on the edge. "What were you dreaming about?"

Should I give her the truth or a load of you-know-what?

"Sophie, sometimes I still dream about my mom… about *losing* my mom." I was glad it was dark enough I didn't have to see the pain I knew was in her eyes.

Sophie nodded just once, and I knew she got the picture.

"Do you ever have dreams… like that?" She knew what I was referring to.

Sophie nodded again, more slowly.

"So you know where I'm coming from, right?"

"Why don't you go take a shower? Then you can sleep in the other bed, where it's dry. I'll get you a drink." It was clear that she didn't want to discuss our mutual childhood abandonment issues that haunted both of our dreams, so she'd changed the subject. And that was fine with me.

So I did as she said, and by the time I was standing outside the bathroom door, shaking some of the water out of my shaggy hair, Sophie was back in my room offering me a cold Sprite.

"Good thing we picked up that minifridge. It was meant for moments like right now." She was really trying to be ultracool about this, when I knew that my dream haunted *her*, as well. It brought all of her own pain back to the front of her mind. And her pain was so much fresher than mine.

"Hopefully, this is a onetime thing, kid."

"You can't control your dreams, I don't think."

She was right about that, so I didn't argue.

Maybe she got a boost of confidence from the darkness between us, but she then managed to surprise me. "What happened in your dream, Phil?"

Since she'd asked so specifically, I figured it was only right that I answer her. Sophie deserved my honesty. "It's a dream that I have over and over, I guess you could say. And it's not so much a 'what happened' kind of dream, as much as it's just a dream about feelings."

We went to the second double bed in my room and sat down beside each other, right in the middle, our legs hanging over the edge. "What kind of feelings?"

I flopped back flat on the bed, and Sophie slid up so that she could lean against the headboard. "I call this kind of 'feelings' dream"—I shrugged away the embarrassment at knowing there were so many different versions that I'd labeled them—"a 'center of attention' dream."

She didn't say anything, so I figured she had no clue what I meant. "When Mom died, I wanted to disappear, and if I couldn't do that, I wanted everybody else to disappear... so that I could be left alone for a while. But it was like there was a conspiracy out there to put *me* in the center of the universe, and everybody and everything had to revolve around me."

"I remember... I mean, I had that feeling sometimes, you know, back when...." Her voice trailed off before she completed her thought.

"I know." I said quickly, struggling to my feet. Enough was enough. "Come on, you need to get back to bed. Ballet at Peridance Capezio Center at nine, right?"

Sophie got up off the bed. "Yeah, and ballet waits for no one." I walked her back to her room. "No more bad dreams, okay, Phil?"

"It's a deal... and none for you either, you hear?"

"I wouldn't *dream* of it." She laughed at her own little joke; Sophie's laughter was a rare, but beautiful, sound that I cherished. "And remember tomorrow night, I have a private lesson with Dario."

"At Battery Dance?"

"Yeah... and we can't be late."

"We were only late that one time... so chill, kid."

"No way—Dario is not a relaxing person to me. And I like it that way. He keeps me *on my toes*—I'm very punny tonight, hmm? But you'll stay in the studio for the lesson, right?"

I suspected that she wasn't ready to be alone in a room with him. But that was not a problem because watching Dario teach Sophie had become a secret hobby of mine. I truly admired his gift of teaching.

"Of course I'll stay. But if you change your mind about that, and you want your old uncle to take a hike, you just tell me, okay?"

Sophie didn't answer, but I figured she was too busy rolling her eyes, although it was too dark to know for sure. She climbed back into her bed.

We had always understood each other in a silent, wordless way. But lately we'd been sharing more of ourselves *out loud*; we'd been chatting almost nonstop at meal times, teasing each other when we were riding on the subway, and tonight, she'd actually come to help me when I was freaking out. This developing closeness to another person, especially in terms of the way we increasingly verbalized our feelings, was odd for me, but it was also rather nice. Smiling, I went back to my room, got into my *second* bed of the night, and pulled back the sheets.

Good night, sleep tight, Philippe—take two!

Some things in my life were good and getting better all the time. I had to be patient with myself and let the rest of it fall into place. But it seemed like I'd been waiting for so long.

EARLY THE next morning, Sophie and I were off to kill two birds with one stone in Union Square—Sophie would take ballet class, *and then* we would explore another dance program—at The Peridance Capezio Center.

Peridance offered a two-year certificate program that Henri had suggested that (okay, he'd commanded) we look into. Sophie already knew that she liked the Peridance ballet classes, and a couple of nights ago, at the end of her lesson, she had shyly asked Dario about the other styles of dance offered there. He had informed her that the modern and contemporary dance teachers at Peridance were among the best in the city. He went on to tell her that he took many classes in the open adult program at Peridance. So today, after Sophie took ballet, we lingered around in the building, observing the comings and goings of the program students. After a while, Sophie worked up the courage to go to the office and request some written information on the certificate program.

"Look, Phil, the certificate program here has a Ballet/Contemporary Track as well as a Commercial Track," Sophie informed me, as she flipped through the paperwork, both of us sitting on a wooden bench in the upstairs lobby.

"What's the story with the Commercial Track?"

"The Commercial Track prepares you for a career on Broadway or for commercial dance work, like being a back-up dancer for a band or for a singer on tour... or to dance on TV, in movies, or even in music videos."

"Sounds cool."

"Cool, maybe—but it's not what I'm looking for. In the other track they offer here, Ballet/Contemporary, they focus on ballet, modern, and contemporary dance. This track prepares you for a career in a dance company."

"Sounds like just what you want."

"And see—" She held out the paper she was looking at. "—I can still do pointe here, and I'd get partnering experience, as well as voice class, too."

She seemed very excited about the certificate program. But I reminded her of Henri's edict. "You'd have to earn a college degree at night or online, though."

"I know... I know... so I have something to 'fall back on,' right?"

I smiled and nodded. And then I yawned.

Those red-eyed masks stole too much of my sleep last night.

But I had still managed to take care of business today, hadn't I?

6

"YOU DID exceptionally well tonight, Sophie. It has only been several weeks since we started, and you do not look like a beginner at modern dance anymore."

Sophie was so psyched up she was just about glowing. "Thank you, D-dario." She was always rather tongue-tied around him, but who was I to talk? I'd never spoken so much as a single syllable to the man, aside from the excuse for our tardiness I'd offered on the night we met.

"Listen, Sophie, I'm substitute teaching a beginner contemporary dance class at Broadway Dance Center tomorrow morning at eleven thirty. I think you should come over and try it out."

"But I've only been doing beginner modern techniques like Horton and Graham. I don't even know what the difference between the modern and contemporary dance is." She sounded a bit whiny.

"Listen carefully to me; you will find that you'll use many of the same techniques that you have learned in traditional modern classes in contemporary class. And Sophie, you are not alone—many people are confused about the difference between the two forms—but *I* consider modern dance to be based in 1900–1950s era and use certain learned techniques, whereas contemporary dance is based in the more current era, like from the 1960s until now and less structured. Many companies overlap from one form to the other, like the Merce Cunningham Dance Company." Dario was always teaching Sophie what he knew about dance history, and she was always eager to lap it up. "But they are both forms of concert dance, and you really should be able to do both. Just come to BDC tomorrow… if you don't like it, you can leave before twenty minutes is over and get your money back."

Sophie's glowing pleasure had toned down some, but she still nodded. "I want to talk to you more about Broadway Dance Center. I haven't been there at all yet."

Those jet black eyes got wide, and he tilted his head as if he was wondering what she was going to ask him.

"Will you come out with Phil and me to get frozen yogurt tonight? And we can talk more then."

Dario didn't answer right away. He turned and then glided to the corner where he'd left his water bottle and backpack. "I didn't bring jeans. I'll have to go like this." He pointed to his black spandex shorts.

That's perfectly fine with me.

"That's okay, Dario. We'd love to have you just as you are. Right, Phil?"

I nodded, meaning it. I took a deep breath and then said, "You've already done so much for Sophie. Let us treat you to some frozen yogurt." And this might seem impossible to believe—it was for me—but Dario and I had never been officially introduced by our full names. He had been all business with Sophie, only, at each and every lesson. So I held my hand out. "I'm Philippe Bergeron, Sophie's uncle and chaperone this summer."

"Uncle?" He was clearly sizing up the lack of difference in our ages. A second later, though, I found myself holding his soft hand, shaking it politely. "Dario Pereira. Pleased to meet you, Philippe." I liked the way he said my name. He put this little "ay" sound at the end that made it sound sexier than usual. "I know a place that has excellent fro-yo not too far from here."

"Sounds great."

Sophie was back to glowing before we were out the door.

WE WALKED a little more than six blocks and found ourselves at a Pinkberry. I was enjoying the best, if not the only, chocolate peanut butter shake I'd ever had, and Sophie was in heaven with her dish of frozen yogurt, covered in fresh strawberries. Dario had gone for a Greek yogurt with all kinds of crunchy mix-ins. He ate it so hungrily that I suspected it might have been his dinner. We'd also gotten lucky and managed to snag one of the few tables available. Sophie and I sat there, both looking to Dario for answers.

"It's just I've heard so much about Broadway Dance Center. It's so famous—always in *Dance Magazine*. Am I really good enough to take class there?"

Dario seemed to have a strict rule of not opening his mouth while there was any food in it. So he didn't answer for a few seconds while he chewed and swallowed. *His* superior etiquette had *me* wiping my beard with a paper napkin almost compulsively. I sure didn't want to disgust him with chocolate-peanut-buttery whiskers.

"Sophie, you are a very talented dancer and could study at BDC year-round if you wanted to. But if it makes you feel any better, over the summer, many high school dance teams take trips to New York City, and so there are always lots of teenagers taking class. In fact, I do a great deal of my substitute teaching over the summers when the regular instructors are off teaching at intensives, so I know what to expect. And you will be fine tomorrow."

"But I heard ballet classes there can be crowded."

"Just stick with the ballet classes that you are used to at Peridance and Steps on Broadway. Just come over to BDC at eleven o'clock tomorrow morning to start stretching for my contemporary class."

"Sophie!" A teenage girl I recognized from Sophie's regular ballet class at Peridance pushed through the door. "OMG! We saw you when we were walking by, girl—come outside and eat your frozen yogurt with us! Me and Jada have iced cappuccinos from Starbucks."

Sophie looked to me, and then to Dario, for permission. I nodded in response, as did Dario, and she was out the door with her girlfriend in a split second, leaving Dario and me alone. I hoped my inner cringing about that fact didn't show.

"I am very impressed by Sophie. She is a strong dancer and a very hard worker."

"I'm pretty sure that she feels exactly the same way about you."

Dario raised his dark eyes from his bowl. "Thank you. That means a lot to me." His lips spoke words of thanks, but his expression remained cynical.

"I hope you don't mind that she can be very... uh, very quiet and shy."

"As can I." He blinked slowly and maybe even blushed a bit. "I have to work at my people skills. Every single day."

I nodded, realizing I'd mistaken his reserved behavior for snobbishness. "I guess the three of us are birds of a feather then." I lifted my hair off of my shoulders with one hand and twisted it in my fingers.

"I can tell that Sophie has been through a lot in her life—I can see it in her dancing—and she emotes very well. But the inner pain I see does not quite fit in with all of the doting-daddy phone calls I've received from Henri Bergeron." His sultry eyes searched mine with interest. "Henri called frequently when we were setting things up for her private lessons, and he still calls quite often to check on her progress... and her happiness."

This man was becoming an important person in Sophie's life, so I decided to trust him. "Her dad, my much older stepbrother, is very protective of her. You see, Sophie's mother and brother passed away in an accident about four years ago. She's struggled a lot with it...they both have."

Dario fell back in his chair. "Oh, I'm so sorry." He clearly meant it.

"I've helped her as much as I've been able to, but there are some things that people have to deal with at their own pace. In any case, I think that dancing has saved her, more than anything else."

I could tell right away that Dario got it, but still, he warned me, "I'm not going to treat her any differently because I know this."

"I wouldn't expect you to."

He got up to throw away his trash. "Would you like me to toss your cup, Philippe?" Again, he said my name with a Latin flair.

"No, thank you. I've got it." I stood, and then we both stepped over to the trash can by the door. I peeked outside to check on Sophie. "I think the girls are finished out there."

Before we headed outside, though, Dario touched my arm tentatively with his fingertips. "Answer one question for me?"

I turned to him and nodded. Curious, yes, but wary, to be sure.

"Why do you hide beneath all of that hair... and the full beard?"

How do I answer that?

"I... I don't know. I just do."

Dario looked away from me like he was again dismissing me, obviously unsatisfied with the answer I'd given. Then he shook his head a couple of times. "I have to go, Philippe. Say goodbye to Sophie for me. I hope to see her in my contemporary class tomorrow."

7

"IT SOUNDS like Sophie is enjoying her time in New York City and being exposed to a variety of new experiences."

I sat in the tiny café at Steps on Broadway, eating a banana, and waiting for Sophie to finish her Beginner Horton Modern dance class. Through trial and error, she had sniffed out a teacher she really liked and felt comfortable with. And from what I saw when I sneaked a peek, which wasn't often because Sophie told me she felt like a little kid dancing for her daddy if I watched too much, she was progressing well. At first, she'd looked like a classical ballerina, trying to force her rigid body into the quirky shapes of modern dance, but lately, she'd started to move more naturally.

"I think she's really taking to the modern classes, but it's a big adjustment for her, Henri."

"How many classes is she taking every week, on average?"

I had to stop and think. "Well, she takes ballet six days… she puts her pointe shoes on for two of those classes. Then there's Pilates and yoga; she alternates those. And she's started to take modern dance class almost every day. First Horton Modern, then Graham, and lately she's been trying out contemporary dance classes whenever Dario, her private teacher, substitute teaches."

"Does she get in a full day of rest every week? That is very important."

"She has, so far. But it's been on different days each week."

"And is she eating well?"

I laughed. "Better than she did at home, I'd say. When dance is particularly frustrating, I take her out for frozen yogurt. I'll put it this way: we go out for frozen yogurt *a lot*."

Henri chuckled, sounding pleased. "And you, Philippe… how are *you* holding up?"

"*Holding up*? What do you mean?" So maybe I *was* a little bit sensitive when he started asking me personal questions. But he'd seen me at my worst, and I knew he had good reason to worry.

"Well, first of all, how is your shoulder?"

A shoulder injury I'd incurred from repetitive motion on the fishing boat is what had gotten me into this whole "summer in the city" situation. Well, my shoulder… and my regard for my niece.

"It's fine. I'm not sure if it's fine enough to pull up nets full of fish, yet."

"It just needs rest… more time off the fishing boat."

"That's what the doctor said. The most physically exerting thing I've done since we've been here is carry my duffel bag to my hotel room."

"No working out?"

"Not really. Soph and I walk a lot. And I try to swim as much as I can, but the hotel pool is crowded so I can't do laps."

"Why don't you join an aquatic club? I told you I'd take care of the cost. It's really not…."

I pulled the phone off of my ear until his voice had quieted. I guess I was sensitive about the fact that Henri insisted on paying for all of my expenses this summer, too. After all, I had managed to save a few dollars over my year and a half of commercial fishing.

"Philippe? Are you listening to me? You are doing a *job*. You're sacrificing your whole summer to chaperone Sophie in the city. You are helping me, and you are helping her… and you know as well as I do that she wouldn't spend a summer in the city with anyone but you or me, and I can't do it thanks to my business."

I really couldn't think of much to say to that. I would do anything to help Sophie and Henri, but it was not as if I had many alternatives. "Well, I'm actually having a decent time here, too." Time for a subject change. "Have you seen Dad?"

"Yeah, I stopped by the home last week. As predicted, he just wanted to know if I brought him cigarettes."

"Then you were dismissed?"

"How'd you guess?"

"I know the man almost as well as you do."

"Not a lot to know there, I don't think, Philippe."

I shrugged. This hadn't been the best idea for a topic, I supposed. My father had always been more or less a figurehead in our family, but never been truly a player in our lives. I shrugged again and mumbled, "Whatever." Which made me feel a lot like Sophie.

Of course, Henri was ready with a new topic. "Are either of you making any friends?"

"Mostly we just hang out with each other. But recently Sophie's made some friends from her dance classes—these girls who come in from New Jersey for ballet."

"And what about you, Phil? Have you made any connections?"

"That's not what I'm here for."

"Sophie is seventeen. She can stay in the hotel room alone if you want to go out some night to have yourself some grown-up fun."

"I'll keep that in mind." A run-and-hide feeling was fast encroaching upon me. I was not into sharing my personal life with my brother. Okay, to be more accurate, I just wasn't *into* having any personal life to share.

I could hear Henri shifting piles of paper around on his desk. "So tell me about Dario Pereira."

My breath caught in my throat. "What do you want to know?" I got up and left the café, heading toward the studio where Sophie was dancing. Class was almost over, and that was when the dancers went across the floor, doing a combination they'd learned. I liked this part the best. Whenever Sophie danced, she was completely enthralled with her movement. Her expression reminded me a lot of Dario's, but she also reminded me more than a little bit of my—

"What's he like?"

"Dario? Um, well, he's great for Sophie. I think he understands her personality. And he gets her to work hard to improve but still feel good about where she is *right now* on her dance path." I searched for Sophie's high blonde ballerina's bun that she still wore to all types of dance classes.

"Soph told me he was 'indecently beautiful.'"

I knew where he was going with this. "She wasn't lying." I found Sophie in the crowd of dancers. She was in the back of the group, as expected, never the first to show her stuff. "He's very handsome, and very good at what he does."

"Any spark between you and him? Soph also tells me he's gay."

This was precisely what I'd expected of my interfering older brother. Henri was always trying to make sure that I was happy. No, his goal went well beyond wanting me to be "happy." My big brother's goal was for me to be *complete*. In fact, it was as if he couldn't rest until Sophie and I were *both* satisfied with life to the fullest. And about Dario having any interest in yours truly, why would he be? No, big brother Henri was not going to be able to satisfy my little crush by tossing cash at it. I stood no chance with Dario Pereira. Not that I wanted one.

"So Phil? Any spark there?"

"Well, anyways, Henri, Sophie's class is almost over. I'll have her call you tonight before bed." I hung up without any further explanations.

Is there a spark between Dario and me?

I was fairly certain that the impeccable Dario found me to be a dirty, disgusting hippy who was heading nowhere in life. And it was sad to say, but he was probably right on the money with that assessment.

8

"WE HAD not intended to exile you from the studio, Philippe, but Sophie wanted the first part of her solo to be a surprise to you. We couldn't very well surprise you if you watched us put it together, could we?" Dario led me back into the studio. I'd been walking around the Upper West Side for the better part of two hours, which I didn't mind in the least—I was just a single grain of sand on the beach, here in this city.

I didn't say anything as I headed toward my usual corner, but Dario stopped me. His wiry arm thrust out across my middle. "Sit up here, instead." He grabbed me by the arm and led me to the front of the studio, and then he pushed me down to sit on the floor with my back against the mirror. Dario had no trouble being pushy.

Sophie took her starting position, and Dario moved to the corner where he started the music, an eccentric blend of bells and chimes and piano. And my niece began to move. The piece seemed to be rooted in ballet, which was clearly Sophie's strongest suit, but Dario had woven into the piece many of the movements she had learned in the different modern and contemporary classes she'd taken since we'd come to the city. I guess he'd been paying attention when she'd demonstrated the different steps she'd learned in classes each day.

My overall impression of the piece—it was stunning—*she* was stunning.

Her body, longer and leaner and stronger than I'd ever before noticed, seemed to own the music. No, it was really much more as if her body was *creating* the music with its movements. She leaned and stretched, her back flat at first and then it gradually curved, and when she leaped, with her feet flexed and her hands posed like claws, I felt goose bumps climb up the skin on my arms.

And Sophie's face reminded me of what I could remember of my mother's. Proud and brave, and, at moments, even tough, but at the very same time, so fragile. But at the moment, she was looking over at me wearing an inquisitive expression, trying to gauge my reaction to the first thirty seconds of her solo. All I could think, though, was that she was everything I remembered my mother being.

"Phil, do you like it?" Her open expression shifted into being one of concern—and it was all Sophie I was seeing again. "Is it okay?"

But my eyes had filled up, and I fought to keep my tears inside. Images of my mother always brought me to this state. I looked to Dario, who now leaned against the far wall, and I saw that he was equally affected by her performance, or maybe it was by my reaction to it. Our damp eyes kind of collided—for a moment it was like we were of one mind—until he nodded a bit in Sophie's direction, to remind me to answer her.

"Was it *okay*? Oh… oh, *shit*, yes." I rarely cursed; my mother hadn't approved of foul language. And then I was somehow up on my feet, looking across the room into her pale blue eyes. "It was… it was amazing, Sophie… I had no idea…." And then I was right beside her. "That dance was beautiful, Soph… *you* were beautiful."

She blushed, pleased and proud. We quickly looked away from each other, though, uncomfortable with the emotion that charged the air between us.

"Well, I guess it's time to call it a night, then." Dario let us off the emotional hook we'd been caught on. He picked up his bag and his water bottle.

Sophie went to the corner to collect her things and checked her phone "Phil, my friends Sara and Emily from ballet class at Peridance invited me to meet them for cookies after my lesson. Can I go?"

Thankfully, her words pulled me the rest of the way out of my memories. After all, I was supposed to be Mr. In-Charge, wasn't I? "Oh, of course you can. Where do they want to meet?"

"At Insomnia Cookies in Greenwich Village."

"Well, tell them you can go, but I have to figure out how to get there first. Um… do you have the address?" I asked her, reaching in my back pocket for my phone.

Dario stepped forward. "I know exactly where Insomnia Cookies is. I'd be happy to take you two there."

"Awesome! Thanks, Dario!" Sophie headed for the door.

"We really appreciate it, Dario. Not just the help getting to the cookie place. But also for the solo because… it was more than I'd hoped for."

For a few seconds, those jet black eyes moved over every inch of my face as if they were reading me. Learning me. "You need to set your hopes higher, then."

I just nodded, no fitting reply coming to my mind, which wasn't particularly surprising.

"The sky is the limit, Philippe, and not just for Sophie." Very curtly, he nodded back at me and followed Sophie from the room.

I HAD to smile—I hadn't seen Sophie chow down on *six* cookies since she and her friends had ambushed the mall's Mrs. Fields Cookies counter at the conclusion of her "shopping birthday party" when she'd turned ten. But there they sat: three ballerinas, hair slicked back into tight buns, wearing "trash bag shorts" on top of pink tights, hovering over a tiny table, shoving chocolate chip cookies into their mouths like there was a shortage of them in NYC. And constantly checking their phones, while laughing a little bit too loud.

Just being teenagers.

"You're crazy about her, aren't you?"

Once again glad for my beard because I was sure that I was blushing to an embarrassing shade of red, I nodded. "You caught me smiling at her, huh?"

"She's very lucky to have an uncle who cares so much." Dario sipped his tea, seemingly a bit caught up in his own thoughts.

"Believe me, I'm just as lucky." I had already scarfed down two cookies and was contemplating a third.

"I believe you." He looked at me very directly, meaning his words.

Tonight Dario's hair was what I'd call messy and boyish. It seemed that he hadn't taken the time to gel it up into its usual tuft-thing. Honestly, he looked hot both ways, like he was a runway model for two different fashion lines, but his hair falling softly around his face like this made me want to touch it.

"Sophie says you're from Somerville."

"She's correct. But it was not the best time of my life, so I don't talk about it a lot. Foster care was… was *challenging* for me."

"You were in foster care? How'd you ever manage to get trained so well in dance? I mean, my brother spends a *fortune* on dance for Sophie. How'd you manage to pay for it as a foster child?" As soon as the question was out of my mouth, I regretted it. I'd been too bold. On impulse, my hand lifted to cover my overly loose lips.

Our eyes met, and I braced myself for his expected annoyance, but he surprised me. His stare was actually less prickly than usual. "Scholarships, mainly. First off, I was very good, and second, boys at ballet schools are always heavily in demand, for partnering."

Dario wasn't the world's most humble man, but if he'd been meek and modest, he probably wouldn't be where he was right now. "So what are you doing now, besides lessons with Sophie?"

I watched as Dario's spine stiffened. He was as every bit as unwilling to share his private life as I was. "In short, I'm doing whatever it takes to make it."

"To 'make it'?"

"I want to end up in a top modern dance company. I don't have enough training yet, and I cannot afford out-of-state college tuition to get it, but the only place I want to be is in New York City so I can audition for all of the notable modern companies. So I share an apartment in Harlem with a number of other dancers, and I work my ass off to pay for it. And in my free time, I take classes. Been at this since I graduated high school a few years ago."

"So when did you graduate from high school?"

"Three years ago in June…and I've been working to build a name for myself here in the city ever since. I'm nearly twenty-two years old, though many people say I look younger."

"You act *much* older."

Dario smiled at me knowingly.

"Do you have any family support at all?"

In an effort to slam the door on *that* topic, the man shook his head hard a couple of times. "There's just me."

I could take a hint. "So where else do you work?"

"A lot of places. I teach ballet and private lessons four days a week in a studio I can easily take a train to in New Jersey. And I substitute teach contemporary dance at BDC, Steps, Peridance, and anywhere else that will have me. I choreograph solos for students of all ages, mostly when I go back to Somerville for visits over the summer. And I perform whenever one of my teachers needs someone to showcase his or her work. I have even been known to clean studio toilets in exchange for classes. As I said, I do whatever it takes."

"Are ends meeting?"

"For the most part." He grinned at me, and his dark eyes sparkled a little; it made him look less stiff and formal than usual. "My roommates and I help each other out when things get tight. We're all in the same boat."

"I'd have bought you a cookie, you know."

The grin dropped right off his lips. "I am not a charity case."

"The solo you're choreographing for Sophie… it's, like, above and beyond the call of duty, Dario. You deserve a *couple dozen* cookies for it." I wasn't kidding.

"It's my job, and Sophie is a very special girl. All she needs is the confidence that she can succeed, and I plan to help her find that. But there will be times when she will not like me as much as she does tonight. I plan to push her very hard."

At least he was honest. "I think you know what the right thing is for her."

After drinking down the rest of his tea, he asked me, "So what's your story, Philippe?"

"My story?"

"Yes. Tell me… I want to know."

Dario had a commanding presence. I realized that as I started to spill out the abbreviated story of my life. "I don't have much of a story, really. Took online and summer classes so I could graduate high school early, and as soon as I turned eighteen the winter before last, I got a job cod fishing out of Gloucester, Mass and fished for well over a year."

"How did you end up in New York City with Sophie?"

"I ask myself that every day." I grinned. "No, seriously, the official story is that I messed up my shoulder and I needed to take some time off fishing to heal it. The real deal is that I'm one of my brother's ongoing projects." Under my beard, once again, my cheeks burned. "And he's relentless."

"*One* of his projects?"

"Yeah… Sophie and me."

"How are you two his 'projects'?"

To buy myself some time to figure out how I was going to phrase my answer, I wiped at my beard with the paper napkin in my hand. "He thinks that if he doesn't get all up in our business, we'll turn into hermits."

Up until that very moment with Dario, only Henri had ever searched my face as if what he saw there *really* mattered. "Is he correct in that theory?"

I had to laugh. "I'd say he's right on the money."

"Then how did you end up here? This is about as far from the peaceful beauty of the ocean as it gets."

"I needed a summer job; Henri needed a New York City chaperone for Sophie. It's that simple."

"Yes, one plus one equals two. And so here you are."

"Henri secretly hopes that both of us will crawl out of our shells while we're here in The Big Apple. He just doesn't get that our shells are the biggest part of us."

Dario tilted his head far off to the left, as if he could understand me better if he examined me from a totally different angle. I sensed his confusion about what I'd just said, and I worried that he might actually get up and leave on me again like he'd done that night at Pinkberry.

So I was more than a little bit surprised when he said, "Philippe, I'd like to take you out for dinner."

All right. I wasn't expecting that. I gawked at him without a word.

"It won't be anything too fancy. But I think I'd like to get to know you better."

Still, I couldn't come up with so much as a word to say.

"We're all done eating, Phil. We'll wait for you guys outside." Sophie and her ballerina friends stood up, and they all looked over at me for my okay.

"Okay... sure. We'll just be a minute." Dario was looking at me, too, and he didn't seem even slightly worried about my lack of response to his invitation.

"So how about tomorrow night... at six?"

"*Hello, Uncle Phil!* Can I meet you outside?" Sophie had asked me something, right?

"I... uh... I have to check it out with Sophie... you know... I have to make sure she won't need me then."

"*Uncle Phil?*"

"Yes, Sophie... I... I'll be outside in a second."

"Where can I pick you up?" That was Dario's voice.

"Um, we're staying at the Holiday Inn on 57th. I can come down to the lobby."

"Perfect."

Without ever saying, "Yes, Dario, I'd like to go out to dinner with you," it seemed that I'd somehow accepted his invitation. "I don't have any fancy clothes."

"I already told you it was not going to be fancy." He stood up and turned to leave without looking at me again.

But I just sat there, staring at him. "Wait... Dario... just... wait just a minute."

He turned around and looked into my eyes with a patience I hadn't expected. "What is it, Philippe?"

Rubbing my forehead with my palm in a futile attempt to settle my brain, I just blurted out, "Are you sure? Are you sure you want to go out with *me*?"

Without hesitation, he replied, "I do... and very much." Try as I might, I couldn't read him. He looked at me blandly, and said, "I'll be waiting for you in the lobby, tomorrow night at six o'clock." And then he left.

9

OKAY, SO here's the real deal: I didn't have much dating experience. In high school, dating hadn't even been an option, as I hadn't been out. But then, I hadn't been much of anything other than "fully entrenched in survivor mode," as my shrink had said, ever since Mom had passed away when I was in fifth grade.

Her death had really messed me up.

It was something of a different story after I'd graduated from high school and started fishing, in that I'd managed to get some anonymous, guy-on-guy action. Always late night, in one or another of the slummy apartments where I'd crashed. In fact, I'd never actually gone out and rented myself an apartment—there had been many available spots on beds, couches and floors in bachelor pads, where I could stay if I bought everybody dinner. In these places, there had also been no shortage of free "love" and drugs of all kinds. I'd never been much into the drug scene, although I realized that with my wild hair and scraggly beard, I certainly looked the part. I was also more than lost enough to play the part of a stoner like I was the genuine article. I'd never been looking for a high, though. All I'd wanted was to just blend in. And I'd blended really well into those slummy hovels.

Back then, the man-on-man action I'd gotten hadn't been pretty or flowery or romantic by any far stretch of the imagination. Emotionally satisfying? Uh, no such luck. Restricted to humping, grinding, and groping each other on top of a pile of coats in a back bedroom, those interactions had served a necessary biological purpose for both of the guys involved. And as soon as our needs had been met, not so much as a single word or even a glance was again exchanged between the participants. Even if it was a repeat hookup.

But here I was, my backside planted on a window-side couch in the lobby of the Holiday Inn on 57th Street, dressed in my only button-down collar shirt, which was for the most part white, and that Sophie had insisted upon ironing, my least tattered pair of cargo shorts, and my single pair of boat shoes. And smelling like Holiday Inn bar soap and shampoo.

Oh yeah, and I wore no backpack. (Sophie had hidden it.)

I felt spiffy enough to be prom-ready.

But I was not so much mentally date-ready—not unless our plan was to find a coat closet somewhere and grind each other into a stupor, as had comprised the full extent of my past experience with dating. And why would the dashing Dario Pereira want a date with yours truly? Maybe I was merely his chosen charity project. Now, *that* made sense.

Just as I expected, Dario stole my breath the very second I caught a glimpse of him as he glided across the lobby in my direction. He looked stylish and polished in a tight black T-shirt and long shorts with those same expensive-looking Italian loafers.

What is he doing here with you, Philippe?

I tried to shut down my inner self-doubt meter, but it was working far too efficiently.

He belongs with a flawless dancer… a picture-perfect prince of the ballet, like the ones I'd seen partnering the ballerinas at Sophie's recitals.

Dario came right up to me and parked himself close by my side. His smell was every bit as mesmerizing as his face and body. It was spicy and sweet but a little bit floral all at the same time.

I looked down into his eyes, and I was immediately aware that he knew just what I was thinking.

"Why are you so convinced that I would want to date a clone of myself, Philippe?"

I had no answer for him.

"Frankly, I would find that very boring." Then he reached up and placed one hand on my bearded cheek, and we looked right at each other. I think we both got a bit caught up in each other's eyes. "Come on, Philippe. Let's go have some fun."

WE PICKED up some sandwiches and drinks at a deli and then took a cab to Central Park. I tried to pay both times, but Dario shut me down, saying, "*I* asked *you* out tonight, Philippe."

By the time we got to Central Park, I was a date-phobic-basket case, and I'm not exaggerating. I had no experience to help me deal with what was going on: a hot guy had picked me up, bought me food, and now, was standing on 59th Street, eagerly engaging a horse and carriage to take me on a ride through the park.

Inside of five minutes, Dario was helping me into an open-topped white carriage, and soon I was being pulled around the park by a stocky gray horse named Muffin. And it was true: the park was very romantic. As we rode, the driver named Billy, pointed out the various landmarks, like the pond, the Wollman ice skating rink—where a kid's carnival was set up, the dairy, and the sheep meadow. At the Bethesda Fountain, Billy stopped so that Dario and I could get out and walk all around it. It was peaceful and breathtaking; I could have stayed there forever. There were lots of people everywhere you looked, but they were just taking in the sights like we were, so I was totally cool with them.

Next, we saw The Dakota, where John Lennon had lived, and we checked out Strawberry Fields with its Imagine ground mosaic, dedicated to Lennon's memory. I had long been a fan of Lennon's music, maybe because we shared an imagine-all-the-people-living-life-in-peace philosophy. So I was thrilled to see this. And Billy was funny and knew a lot about a lot; he shared his inside info on many of the movies that had been filmed in Central Park, and he told us all about the famous people he'd seen jogging around.

I was thankful for Billy's nonstop jabbering. So much so, that I could've kissed the man. He took the pressure off me, in the sense that I didn't have to worry about being charming, or funny, or anything else, when it came to Dario. All I had to do was sit on the bench and take it all in—there were no expectations of me. But even while Billy pointed out the different statues and rattled off his little "once upon a time in Central Park" stories, Dario's attention was focused 100 percent on me. His dark eyes followed my every movement, and although he somehow managed to laugh at all the right moments and glance at the points of interest when directed, it was obvious that, for him, I was this carriage ride's feature attraction. And you know what? That realization had me shifting around awkwardly on the hard cushion of the carriage's bench seat.

After the ride, which once again Dario wouldn't let me pitch in any money toward, we almost instinctively found our way back to the

Bethesda Fountain, and then we grabbed a spot to sit at the pool's edge. For a while we both studied the huge statue of an angel at the fountain's center in silence.

"Here, Philippe." Dario handed me my sandwich from the brown paper bag he carried. Then he gallantly opened my bottle of iced tea, as if I wasn't capable of doing it for myself. After he did that, when he winked at me, I felt warm inside. Like maybe he was looking out for me.

"Thanks." The time had come for making small talk. So I decided to unwrap my sandwich and take a big bite, which would necessarily delay our conversation.

"So how do you like New York City?" He opened up his own sandwich and took a perfect-sized bite: not too big and not too small. Just right.

I wiped at my beard with my sleeve but stopped short when I realized what I'd just done. (Fishermen weren't exactly obsessed with the rules of proper etiquette.) "I like it right here. *Right now.*"

Dario smiled at me. "Good answer." He was still looking at me like he wanted me to say more, which didn't surprise me much. "But what I mean is, overall, do you like the city?"

"That depends. Do you want me to give you an answer you'll like, or do you want me to tell you the truth?"

He tilted his head, trying to figure out what I'd meant. "The truth, of course."

"One night, when I told you the truth, you got up and left me."

"Are you referring to when I asked you why you hide behind all the hair and you said you didn't know?"

"Yeah… that night at Pinkberry."

"I left because you *do* know why you hide. Your answer to my question was not truthful."

He had me there, which caused me to blush, something I'd been doing way too much lately. "Okay, so you want to know if I like New York City, and I do. I'm kind of surprised by that, too, because I've always been so into nature, especially wide open spaces like the ocean."

"And why do you think this crowded city works for you?"

I rubbed my beard several times with a flattened palm, and then I grabbed a fist full of my long hair, pulled it up off my neck, holding it there until I felt the breeze kiss the backs of my ears. "Because I like to hide, and hiding's easy here."

"It's also easy to get lost in the crowd."

He said it like it was a *bad* thing. "Yeah, that too."

"You *want* to get lost in the crowd?"

"Most of the time, I do." I looked at him directly. After all, hadn't he told me he'd wanted the truth?

Dario took a deep breath, blew it out harshly, and clenched his fists, like he was fighting an urge to shake me. "I spend my entire life *trying* to stand out in a crowd. If I cannot stand out in a group of dancers, I will never get a job in the dance world."

"I guess we're very different."

"In some ways. But I never said that I *liked* to stand out, just that I have to. That's why I work so hard to be the best dancer I can be, so I will stand out in a way I'll be proud of."

I nodded my understanding.

"And be warned: you stand out quite a lot to me, Philippe." He continued to watch me, but now his gaze felt soft and warm. And focused... very focused.

Which made my face heat up again. "Uh... thank you, Dario, but I'm not at all sure why that is."

Dario tugged my sandwich from out of my hands and stuck his own sandwich down beside mine on the paper bag. "I have never met anyone like you. I work in the entertainment field, which can be very superficial, Philippe, and you are just... just so incredibly genuine. It shows in every small detail—mostly in your eyes—but also in your personal style, the way you care for Sophie, even in your overgrown beard, which I, incidentally, love. I left Pinkberry that night because I couldn't stand to hear you intentionally mislead me—because you *do know* why you hide. You may not be ready to tell me your reasons yet, but you know what they are."

I couldn't think of a reply, probably because of the small fact that what Dario had just said was so true. I'd never told anyone of how badly

I'd suffered over my mother's death... how I still suffered the loss of her. Only Henri knew because he had been there from beginning to end to witness the whole ugly scene.

But the fact that I was tongue-tied did not seem to dismay him. "I'm hoping we share just enough in common to make us compatible, and at the same time, we differ sufficiently that we will be fascinating to one another."

Nodding, I admitted to something pretty significant, at least it was for me. "I'm already pretty much fascinated with you, Dario." I felt that frequent blush taking its usual place on my cheeks.

The look in his eyes showed the pleasure he felt at my sincerity. And in his next breath he admitted a truth to match mine. "I want to kiss you."

So maybe I nodded again.

Dario leaned in toward me, lifted up his perfect lips to mine, and all I could think when they touched together was "so soft." I was pretty sure he liked kissing me, too, judging by the way he reached around my neck, pulled my face down toward his, and kissed me some more.

I just couldn't stop myself from grinning when our lips came apart, and Dario laughed out loud when he saw my huge smile, because I know he didn't expect it from someone as reserved as me.

He spoke softly. "You are a very special man."

And that was enough to turn my grinning lips into a straight line, because hearing compliments had made me uncomfortable for as long as I could remember.

But before I had a chance to worry about what to say next, Dario was thrusting my sandwich back into my hands. "Don't think I'm finished with you when that sandwich is gone. There is real, full-fat ice cream on our evening's agenda, if you promise not to tell Sophie."

Before I even had a chance to make that promise, I got kissed again.

10

IT HAD become a habit: morning swimming whenever Sophie took more than two dance classes in a row at the same studio.

"We *must* stop meeting like this, Phil." Lauren shook out her towel so that it covered the entire length of her lounge chair, and then she stuck her canvas bag filled with Tommy's towel and brand new swim goggles, and whatever other things a little boy needed for a morning spent by the pool, on the chair beside me.

"Good morning, Lauren." Tommy was already by the pool's ladder, dipping his toes in the water to check the temperature.

"Not so crowded today." She looked up at the cloudy sky. "Hey, Tommy, what did you do with the sun?"

Tommy turned toward us and grinned. "I stuck it under my bed."

We both laughed.

"Where's Sophie this morning?"

"At Peridance Capezio Center. She really likes to dance there; she says it's very professional but low-key. And there are a couple of girls in the classes who she's made friends with." I stood up because Tommy was already sending me his "What's taking you so long?" look. "I'll pick her up this afternoon."

"Your niece is so beautiful, Phil. I'd just love to see her dance sometime." Sophie had come up to the pool with me a couple of times. She'd been crazy about Tommy. He could've been her little brother; Sophie and Tommy looked so much alike with their white-blond pool-water-soaked hair.

I froze right where I stood when I realized what I'd just thought. Sophie's little brother, Stefan, was about Tommy's age when he was in the car accident. And he'd been every bit as blond and adorable as Tommy.

"You okay, Phil?" Lauren had popped upright on her lounge chair and was looking concerned. "Please don't think you *have* to swim with Tommy. It's not your job."

Pulling myself from out of my dark thoughts, I turned back to Lauren. "No... no, I love swimming with Tommy. I look forward to it, believe me." I lowered my voice. "I was just thinking about my nephew... Sophie's little brother. We... uh... we lost him to a car accident about four years ago, when he was five."

Why on God's green Earth am I telling her this?

The last thing this young mom needed was to be forced to deal with my emotional baggage. I was sure that with the divorce she had plenty of her own baggage to keep her mind occupied.

"I'm so sorry." She looked pained. "Do you think it bothered Sophie to see Tommy here? I can keep him away next time she comes to the pool with you?"

I shook my head. "Oh, no... I think it's more the opposite. I think that playing with Tommy brings back memories of happy times with Stefan. I'm sorry... I really shouldn't have told you all that."

And suddenly Lauren was on her feet right in front of me, hands on her hips. And looking mighty angry. "Philippe Bergeron, I consider you to be a friend of mine. In fact, I've only known you for three weeks, but I already like you better than any of the women I ever met at the country club pool back in South Carolina."

Where is she going with this?

"I've unburdened on you about how much this divorce has taken out of me, how much I miss working, about Tommy's issues with bedwetting, about how difficult it was to find an apartment, just to name a few things. I would be extremely hurt if you didn't unburden yourself on me, as well. Phil, we're *friends*...."

And you know what? I believed her, just because of the way her eyes had gotten a bit wet in the corners. "Thanks for saying that, Lauren. I think of you and Tommy as my friends too." Sure, it had been hard to say, as I wasn't one for emotional declarations, but I'd known that it had to be said anyhow. I pried one of her hands from her hip and squeezed it.

I thought I saw relief in her eyes. "And Tommy misses his father; he travels all the time. I think he really enjoys spending time with a young man who cares about him, like you do."

Okay.... It was way past time to lighten up the mood around here. In a loud voice, I asked, "So where *is* that little dolphin? When I find him, I'm gonna toss him into the water!" I turned and looked around like I couldn't find Tommy anywhere, when he was right under my nose.

"Here I am, Flip! Betcha can't catch me!" *Splash!* The little guy was in the water, T-shirt and all.

I looked to Lauren, worried that the kid had gotten his shirt wet. "Don't worry about it, Phil, I have three more shirts for him in my bag." She picked up her cell phone and went to work on whatever it was she was currently obsessed with. I thought that maybe she was job-hunting, something I was going to need to do in the fall if my shoulder was still messed-up and I couldn't return to fishing, which was Henri's greatest wish for me. He told me all the time that he prayed I'd find my calling somewhere other than out on the dangerous ocean, as he didn't want to lose any more family members.

I was in the pool within a split second, chasing Tommy around and feeling pretty happy with life.

11

"I *AM* trying, Dario!" Sophie wiped her forehead dramatically with her wrist. "See this?" She held out her wet wrist for his inspection. "It's called sweat! And it's here on my forehead because I'm working as freaking hard as I can!"

Dario didn't say even a word back to her; he just looked at her like she was a specimen of contaminated ground water bottled-up in a test tube. "I was going to ask you to try it again, but I have a better idea. You go take a break—stop *sweating* for a while, since you dislike it so much. Your *uncle* can take a stab at it. He could not suck any more than you just did."

I swore that steam was coming out of Sophie's ears. "I have to go to the bathroom!" She made a hasty exit.

Dario and I looked at each other.

"I don't actually have to try to do a barrel turn, do I?" I wouldn't put much of anything past Dario when he was trying to make a point with Sophie.

"No... I was just trying to piss her off." His wide eyes looked really innocent, considering the circumstances.

"Why on God's green Earth would you want to do that? It isn't a pretty sight at all when Soph is mad; she turns bright red, sweats like a lumberjack, and I'm expecting foul language to spurt from out of her lips at any moment."

"Philippe, you have got to understand: Sophie is the type who, the angrier she gets, the more focused she gets." Dario bent over to pick up his water bottle and then took a long swig. "You'll see." I had to say, he wore his confidence well.

My niece stormed back into the room. Without a single word, she got into this bent over position and snapped, letting Dario know that she was ready to start, and then went on to do three perfect barrel turns, right in a row.

Dario took another long sip of water. "Not bad. But can you do that again?"

Way beyond reasonable words, Sophie eyed Dario, none too kindly. "Take notes on how it's done, mister."

I could tell that Dario was stifling a strong urge to smirk. "Maybe I will."

She bent back over and did three more perfect turns. Then she stood upright, stuck her hands on her hips with no shortage of snarky attitude, and turned to me. "Your turn, *Uncle Phil*." As if *I* had been part of a conspiracy against her.

When I started to protest, Dario cracked up into a fit of laughter. "Yeah, *Uncle Phil*... let's see what you've got!"

"I'll meet you guys out front." I was gone before those two could blink.

A couple of minutes later, they came out of the building. Sophie trotted over to the nearby food cart on the sidewalk to get a drink.

"I don't think she was being lazy, you know, back in the dance studio." It *was* my job to defend her, right? Plus, Sophie could never be accused of being a lazy dancer—that just wasn't her.

"Oh, no. I never thought that."

I looked at him blankly. "You told her that she wasn't trying. I heard you...."

He chuckled a little and then leaned in toward me like he had a big secret. "Yeah, maybe that *is* what I *said*, but it was *not* what I actually *meant*."

He'd officially lost me.

"Sophie was busy convincing herself that she couldn't do it, and that was because she was so overly focused on the step, itself. I decided to give her something else to focus on—being pissed at yours truly."

Dario could possibly be an evil genius.

"So I told her that she was being lazy and was not trying hard enough, thus, giving her something else to focus her frustrated mind on...

and what do you know? She came back in the studio and nailed it. Six times."

Dario Pereira is definitely an evil genius.

"Are you two still on speaking terms?"

Dario glanced over at her. She was coming toward us with a Diet Snapple for herself and one for Dario, too. "Oh, yeah, we're fine. In fact, Sophie is on cloud nine. She loves me."

"Here, Dario… I got you a drink." It looked like Dario was correct in how he'd handled her.

"Thanks, Sophie. I am so proud of what you accomplished in there today."

Sophie didn't say anything, but she *did* kind of resemble the cat that swallowed the canary.

"Next lesson, though, I'm devoting fifteen solid minutes to teaching your uncle to do a proper barrel turn. We're not going to let him off the hook without a fight, right?"

They pressed their heads together, snickered a bit, and took off toward the deli on the corner where we'd planned to eat lunch. I trailed behind them, shaking my head, absolutely sure that I'd missed something huge.

12

THE STATE University of New York at Purchase had an upscale, grassy, suburban feel, and it wasn't too far outside of the city. Maybe just far enough for someone to focus on school, but not too far to keep from making use of all the opportunities in the big city. Plus Dario had given SUNY Purchase two big thumbs up, saying that if he'd been able to go to college out-of-state, it would have been his top choice.

And I'll admit, when touring this school with Sophie—*for Sophie*—I had to push images of me walking around campus, my JanSport backpack filled with schoolbooks, out of my mind. I found that just plain strange considering how I'd broken my back taking extra classes to finish high school early so I wouldn't have to attend a structured school any longer.

Since the Conservatory of Dance tours were only given during the school year, Sophie and I took a general tour of the campus. Both of us got into the overall artsy feeling of the school, and we could see that there were plenty of opportunities for the students there to display their performance and artistic skills. Sophie also went crazy over the "Stood" or the Student Center, which was a totally student run rec complex, where the kids went to burn off a little bit of their excess studying steam. The Stood also had another superinnovative thing going on: the walls were covered in student-painted murals. Even though we couldn't go for the actual dance tour, Dario had told us that Purchase offered superior ballet every day of the week and the opportunity to do pointe, and also that the modern program at SUNY was top-notch. He'd actually gone online to the SUNY Purchase website, printed out the list of its dance alumni performing in major companies, and brought it along to show us at Sophie's last private lesson. The list was pages long.

We sat in the Starbucks on campus, waiting for the taxi that would take us back to the White Plains train station, when Sophie finally spoke. "I really like it here. Maybe too much. I'm scared I won't be accepted, you know?"

"Well, first of all, Dario said he thinks you have what it takes to be accepted here because your ballet is so strong. And second, isn't that a big part of the reason we came here to the city this summer—to take a lot of modern dance classes to prepare you for your college audition?"

She crossed her long legs. "Yeah, I know."

"And if you don't *try* to get in, you definitely won't be accepted, right?"

Soph was fidgety. She uncrossed her legs and then tucked them beneath her on the puffy chair. "I know that too. But my friends Sara and Emily from Peridance are also gonna try to get in here, and they're so much better than me at modern dance."

"They just have more experience, that's all." I sipped my coffee without taking my eyes off her.

"But they live near the city and can keep taking modern throughout the fall. I'm going back to Cambridge to take straight ballet. There's no way I'll be ready in the winter to audition in modern dance."

"Then I'll take you back to New York City every couple weekends in the fall right up until college auditions to keep you up on modern dance." I couldn't believe I was saying what I was saying, but Sophie being happy meant more to me than getting lost in the stars out on the Atlantic ever could. "We'll make it work, Soph, don't worry."

The smile she sent me would make cutting off a limb worthwhile. Her pale skin got brighter, and I felt like her hero. "You so rock, Phil."

13

IT WAS August and our time in New York City was halfway over. I wasn't too sure how I felt about that.

Sophie was almost like a new dancer; her body had finally taken to the contracting and releasing movements of contemporary and modern dance. She also seemed incredibly happy in the hectic atmosphere of this big city. Sophie had developed a regular routine: every day, she took Pilates or yoga, ballet class, modern and/or contemporary class, and she accomplished this by traveling to different studios all around the city. She knew the subway routes, the places she liked to eat, and she had made friends she could relate to. What I thought was really sweet was that she'd recently started to dress with a bit of a personal style, as she never had before. Dancer-hippy-chic, I guess you could call it. And as of that week, we'd started renting empty studio space so that she could practice what she'd learned, to this point, of her college audition solo. Sophie wanted to surprise Dario with how well she'd polished it in the time that he was away.

I hadn't seen Dario in the five days since our date. He'd gone back to Massachusetts to teach dance solos to competition kids he knew from growing up in Somerville and anybody else who had gotten their hands on his business card and had the cash. Before leaving, he'd told me that these solos were his "bread and butter." They paid for a good part of his living expenses in New York City. He taught these solos at a couple of different studios outside of Boston in the summer, but mainly at the studio he'd gone to in high school, cranking out about three pieces each day that he was home. Then at Thanksgiving, he checked in on his students' progress, and over Christmas break, he polished the routines so that they were all ready to perform for the competition dance season.

Honestly, I couldn't say I'd missed him when he was gone. It had taken me the first two days after our date for me to recover from the shock of having had a real date in the first place, the third day I spent deciding whether or not I'd liked the one-on-one attention Dario had showered on me, and after deciding that I'd liked the special treatment from Dario, the next two days had been spent questioning every move I'd made and every word I'd said on our visit to Central Park.

Did I come across as awkward as I felt? Did I talk with food in my mouth? Was I, in any way, witty and/or charming? Did I thank him enough? Did my kisses suck?

Will we ever go out again? That was the big one.

Is it my turn to ask him out? But this was the one I suffered over the most.

So, as could have been predicted, I was a bit wound up by the time the night came for Sophie's next private lesson. I didn't go inside the studio; instead, I just dropped Sophie off and ran like hell to hide among the hordes of people on the street.

At least that had been the plan, but on my way down the first flight of stairs, I heard Dario's voice ringing down from up above. "Philippe, come back upstairs, please. I need to talk to you."

Hello, Philippe! You are Sophie's guardian—the responsible one, right?

Her dance teacher needed to talk to me, and I was hightailing it out of there like I was being chased. So I stopped, but I didn't turn around.

"Philippe, please." It was a demanding sort of "please."

I turned around and climbed back up the flight I'd almost fully descended.

When I was finally standing in front of him, Dario looked at me directly, but he didn't appear worried or confused, which honestly baffled me. In fact, the guy looked like he totally understood what was going on with me—that I'd been fleeing all of my fears and doubts and worries about *him*.

"Come here, Philippe."

So I stepped over to him, right into his space. He reached up and pulled me against him with those strong dancer's arms. His hands found my beard, and then my hair, and soon they were locked around my neck.

And then he looked up at me with those alluring jet black eyes and told me, "I missed you while I was away, Phil." He'd never called me Phil before. He'd been so formal, always using "Philippe".

I looked down at him and nodded, not sure as to whether or not I should agree.

"Let's go out for something to eat after Sophie's lesson. I just got back to town, and I am famished."

I nodded again, this time getting a bit lost in his pretty eyes. And he smiled, like he knew.

Right away, my worries vanished.

Then Dario took hold of my hand and led me back into the dance studio where Sophie was stretching at the bar. She glanced over at us, our hands clasped tightly together, and rolled her eyes. Then Dario pushed me down onto a metal chair in the corner and got back to the business at hand.

THE THREE of us found ourselves at one of the many hole-in-the-wall café/buffet/deli/grocery stores that you could find on every block in NYC. We'd all built enormous salads at the salad bar and gotten iced mocha lattes to drink. Finally, we'd parked ourselves in the customer seating area at the back of the building. Sophie was texting her new friends rather madly, and Dario and I were sizing each other up across the table.

"How was your trip home?"

"Well, it was not so much a trip 'home' as it was a business trip. I stayed with the owner of the dance studio that I attended during high school. Lacy is the one who lines up the majority of my solos for the students in her own studio."

"How many solos did you choreograph?"

"Sixteen… and everybody paid in full. I feel like a rich man."

That was cute. "I thought a lot about our… uh, our date… the other n-night."

He tilted his head in that curious way he had. "I did too."

I wanted to shake him and shout, "What *exactly* did you think, Dario? Spill it, buddy! And I want details…." but I managed to hold back.

What I *did* ask him was, "C-could I take you out this w-weekend? Sophie is going to sleep in New Jersey at her friend's house on Saturday night, so I'm free... I mean, if you're free... and...."

"Yes."

"You want to?"

"I said yes, *didn't I?*" He was still examining me like I was some kind of an oddity showcased at Ripley's Believe It or Not! in Times Square. "Let me meet you at your hotel again. I have classes in the afternoon at Steps—I'm going to take ballet in the late morning, Horton Modern, and then there is a Broadway Tap class that I really enjoy—and I can shower there and meet you after at your hotel."

"No, it's okay. I'll meet you at Steps on Broadway, in the lobby. What time is your class over?"

"At four thirty, but I'll need a half hour to shower and get dressed."

"I'll be there no later than five then."

Dario smiled. I wondered if he knew how difficult it had been for me to ask him out. I suspected that he did. He seemed to be able to read me like a book.

"I will be looking forward to it, Phil."

14

MAYBE IT was lame, but I decided to take Dario to Madame Tussauds wax museum and then out to dinner at the Hard Rock Cafe. *How much more touristy can I get?* But I'd checked with Sophie, and she'd told me that Dario had said he'd never seen the wax figures and always wanted to.

I sat on one of the long narrow wooden benches on the third floor of Steps on Broadway, wearing the second nicest outfit I owned—which had been Sophie-inspected and reluctantly approved. Pretty much all I had with me were cargo shorts and T-shirts, but I'd found this pair of colorful Madras-patch Bermuda shorts and a white Ralph Lauren polo shirt wrinkled up on the bottom of my duffel bag. The night before, Sophie had hand washed them using her shampoo for soap and then hung them to dry in the shower. When I'd left her at the train to go to New Jersey this morning to sleep over at her new friend Sara's house, she'd kissed my cheek and told me I looked good, but in a "wrinkled, preppy" way.

Preppy? Me? Right. I guess all I needed was one of those embroidered whale belts, a Jack Kennedy haircut, and a close shave, and I'd look the part of *prep boy goes sailing*. I mean, I even had my boat shoes on to complete the look. And no beat-up black backpack strapped onto my shoulders, as Sophie had made me promise I'd leave it at the hotel.

When I saw Dario, the first thing that crossed my mind was that we were going to be hitting the streets of New York City looking like a page from the J. Crew Summer Catalog. He, of course, didn't have the air-dried-in-the-shower-wrinkled-excessively-hairy-look going on, but he sure looked preppy, with a pinstriped button-collar shirt, knee-length navy shorts, and even a sweater tied around his neck. And it was boat shoe night all-around.

I stood up from the wooden bench, planning to give him a big hug, when a gracefully walking, smooth-talking male dancer approached us.

"Don't tell me you took tap class again, Dari. I saw your bag in the locker room, but you, my dear, were nowhere to be found." The tall blond man in black tights and a white T-shirt leaned in toward Dario and kissed him on one cheek and then the other.

Dario pushed the guy back a bit and said, "Yes, I was downstairs… in Advanced Broadway Tap."

"Why do you waste your time down there when you could be up here shaking your stuff in Broadway Jazz, hmm?"

"You know I love tap. It's classic. And it keeps my rhythms sharp."

The blond rolled his eyes in a manner that reminded me of Sophie and then combed his fingers through his hair. Neither of them had so much as looked my way my at this point, so I just sat back down. I was out of my element, and I had the sense to know it.

What am I doing here with these upscale people?

Dario frowned down at me. He then reached out his hand just a bit, and if I wanted to take it, I had to stand back up, so I did. "Kenny, please meet my date tonight, Philippe Bergeron. Philippe, this is Kenny Larson. He and I take many of our classes together."

Kenny leaned against Dario's side like he owned him, and Dario released my hand. "In other words, we're pretty much *always* together… as in, attached at the hip." He then looked squarely at Dario. "You never told me you were into *bears*, Dari."

For the first time since I'd met him, Dario appeared flustered. "Kenny, you need to shut up." He said it with a smile, but I knew that he really did want Kenny to zip his lips.

Am I a bear?

If I was a bear, it wasn't really by philosophy or intention, not that I had anything against the mega-masculine bear culture in the LGBT community. It was more that I liked to have a barrier between the world and me—lots of hair did the trick.

I stood there staring at the two beautiful men in front of me, wondering why Dario wasn't all dressed up and ready to go out to a Broadway show with Kenny Larson, here, instead of with "Philippe the Bear." And both of my hands rose up to my beard like they were being controlled by invisible strings, and they started tugging—an unfortunate, and quite painful, nervous habit of mine.

But after a couple of seconds, I found the presence of mind to hold out my hand to Kenny, and when he reluctantly took it, I said, "I... um... I'm pleased to meet you, Kenny."

Kenny gaped down at our hands as they clasped together. "Revolted" would sum up his expression. Or "fearful that he'd catch something" would work equally well.

"Well, we have got to be on our way, Kenny. Have a good night." Dario snatched my hand again, in that bossy way he had, and led me a couple of steps toward the door.

But neither of us could miss it, no matter how much we might have wanted to. In fact, I don't think anyone in the entire lobby missed it. "Are you for real, Dario? You're really going out with *that Sasquatch*?"

I didn't wait around to hear Dario's answer. I bolted to the stairs.

Fuck the elevator—I was out of there!

"PHIL... PHILIPPE... wait!"

I could hear Dario's voice a flight above me and getting closer. And normally, I'd do as he said and wait, as I was usually obedient to anyone who issued an order to me. But since I wasn't used to putting myself out there like I was doing with Dario to start with, and then to have Kenny... to have Kenny say that stuff... well, I was *so* out of there. When I heard Dario call out to me, I didn't even slow down a bit.

"So this is how you treat your date? One bitchy dude says something that rubs you the wrong way, and you take off on the person you have plans with?"

I stopped.

Apparently, he'd stopped, too, because his voice wasn't coming any closer to me. "That's fine. I'm glad I know that about you now."

I turned. And it took everything I had in me to drag my feet back up the stairs.

But I did it.

Dario stood on the landing of the second floor with a hand on his hip. He still looked flustered, and I'd say he looked angry too. I shrugged, partly because I was so nervous, and partly because I had no clue as to what he expected me to say.

But Dario, as usual, seemed to know just what to do. He reached out his arms toward me, pulled me against him, and said right into my ear, "You are incredibly beautiful, Philippe." And when he traced his fingers along both of my cheekbones, I believed that he meant what he'd just said. "So handsome... maybe even pretty under that beard... and so kindhearted." I searched his eyes for the strength I needed to keep going with tonight's date. "Philippe, I want to be with you tonight." I wasn't sure just what he meant by that.

I shook my head again and spoke quietly. "Sorry about bolting."

Staring at my lips, Dario's fingers moved down from my cheeks until they were smoothing over my mouth. I knew he was going to kiss me. He leaned forward, and I bent down just enough to allow it to happen. And it was like I was filled with his strength through that kiss.

He exhaled with satisfaction, his minty breath blowing against my lips. "So where are you taking me tonight?"

And quick as that, everything was all right again. Next thing I knew, I was telling him about how we were going to see President Obama at Madame Tussauds wax museum.

IN THE Hard Rock Cafe, we sat right at the base of Ringo Starr's drum set. Which was something else, I have to say. We stared at each other across the table over tall glasses of iced tea, offering our opinions as to what we thought of the wax museum. The restaurant was just dark and crowded enough for me to really be able to relax.

"I think my favorite was Madonna," Dario said. "Closely followed by Anderson Cooper." He looked a little bit dreamy-eyed, but Anderson Cooper had that effect on lots of people. "Which ones were you most impressed by?"

"I liked President Obama. And Abraham Lincoln too."

"Are you an extremely political person?" He looked at me in that way he had, his head tilted.

"No, not really. I just like it that Obama stood up for gay marriage. And Sophie, Henri, and I saw that movie about Abraham Lincoln before we came to New York City… with Daniel Day-Lewis. Loved it."

"Well, thank you for taking me there. I've been in The Big Apple for two years, and it was starting to get embarrassing to admit that I had never been to Madame Tussauds."

"I was going to see if you wanted to go to a Broadway show, but I had no idea which one to choose."

Dario smiled at me. "I would love to see a show with you someday. I've heard a lot about *Annie* from my students in Somerville. They came and saw it over Christmas break last year, and then we got together at some studios here and worked on their solos. After seeing *Annie*, the kids were motivated to get to work, let me tell you."

"If we ever see *Annie*, would you mind if Sophie tagged along? I can remember her watching that movie on DVD when she was a little kid."

His smile grew. "Of course she can come. Sophie's great." Dario took a sip of iced tea, spilling a drop on his chin. His little pink tongue darted out to catch it, and I felt a surge of desire that really surprised me. "I love how you care about her so much, Philippe. You are very dedicated to the people who are close to you, hmm?" He thought for a minute, and then added, "But there are very few who you let inside your shell."

He was right on both counts so I nodded.

"I hope you are willing to take a chance on me."

I was locked inside his gaze. "I think I already have, don't you?"

"But you were so quick to take off on me today when Kenny was being a douche."

I placed my drink back down on the table, embarrassed, as I should be. "I'm sorry."

"I don't want you to be sorry. I want to know what you were thinking."

But there was the problem, because I didn't want to think about my feelings, let alone discuss them.

What man really wants to analyze why he has so little self-confidence that he can't tell a sorry loser like Kenny to take a hike when he's out of line?

"So tell me. What happened *inside your head* at Steps on Broadway... when you ran for the stairs? I heard what Kenny said, but what I'm interested in is why you reacted by retreating instead of punching him out."

I wanted to say that I didn't know why I'd bolted. But I *did* know.

He won't put up with lies. He'll leave me if I don't come clean.

"If you don't want to tell me about it then just say so."

"I... uh...."

It was like I could feel his stare probing at my brain.

Pressing and pushing and urging me to open up.

"I want you to be able to talk to me, Philippe. *Please....*"

"I... I'm afraid... that if I do... talk to you, that is... you'll *see me.*"

He didn't say anything to that confession. He just looked at me with his head tilted to the side, which made me even more insecure about the turn our conversation had taken.

"You know, that you'll really *see* me and not... not like what you see."

"And then what would happen, Philippe?"

"If you didn't like what you saw, then I would know for sure that I shouldn't have let you see me in the first place."

"And then... then what? What could possibly be so bad?"

I shifted around on my chair, trying to find a comfortable position, which wasn't happening, so I took a minute to focus my mind on Ringo's drums, hoping to center my thoughts. "It doesn't hurt to be invisible, Dario. But it hurts me to be stared at... and it hurts the most to be left alone, even if it is exactly what a certain part of me wants. So if you're *really* looking at me, as in, closely, and you don't like what you see, then I get both things I always try so hard to avoid. I get exposed... and maybe deserted." It all spilled out in a convoluted spurt, didn't it? And I waited for a rush of regret about letting Dario see all of the turmoil that was rushing around in my head. Weird thing was, it didn't come.

The waitress, however, did come. All cheerful and bright-eyed, she chirped, "Here, sir, is your Grilled Norwegian Salmon and your Blackened Chicken Pasta. Please be careful, the plates are both very hot. Now, can I get you boys anything else?"

I looked to Dario, and he shook his head at me, and so I, in turn, shook my head at her. Then I mentally kicked myself for being unable to come up with anything polite to say to her, and forced a smile.

"Well, then enjoy your dinner."

Steam from the entrées rose up between us. The food smelled great, and the way the opposite scents blended together only made it smell better. But neither of us reached for our silverware.

"Thank you for telling me that. I'm sure it was not easy. Now tell me what you were thinking when you took off today, at Steps on Broadway."

Drops of sweat rolled down the sides of my face. I felt naked, as I had so often as a child. But still I answered him. "His words got me noticed, stared at, even, by everyone in the lobby... and by you. And at that very moment, I felt like nothing was worth the feeling of being spotted and gaped at."

Only after Dario picked up his silverware, did he finally set me free of his gaze. "Sometimes, Phil, you need to take a risk in life." He stuck his napkin on his lap and then drove his fork into his rice. "Maybe you should look at it this way, if you never take a risk by putting yourself out there, you'll keep on getting what you've always gotten. But if you *do* take a chance on something, or on someone—like me, for example—that is when amazing things can happen."

I sat there beneath Ringo's drum set, frozen with the shock that I'd really opened my heart enough to tell Dario one of my secrets, and yeah, I was also scared that I wanted so badly to take a risk on this man. "I'll try."

Dario looked up. In the past thirty seconds, he'd unbuttoned, and then rebuttoned the collar of his shirt three times, like he was nervous too. "You will?"

"I want to take a chance with you. But I'm scared that Kenny might have been right—that I'm not good enough for someone like you. And maybe it would be easier to just stay invisible." I had no idea where I'd found the courage to be so honest. It was unlike me, but I supposed that maybe I'd decided Dario was right, and it was time to take a risk. If anyone was worth it, he was.

Dario's sudden anger caught me off guard. "Kenny's just a jealous bitch! He would love to be with a man as beautiful and sweet and genuine as you. But he knows that he doesn't stand a chance with someone of your sensitivity and beauty… and of your quality."

I took my own silverware in hand and unwrapped it from the napkin. I tried so hard not to shake my head to deny his words, confident in my belief that he was mistaken about me.

"But, Philippe, you just told me that you are going to risk feeling the things you fear the most, for *me*. It looks like I have somehow managed to win the jackpot, haven't I?" He smiled warmly, the way he had earlier. "Now, don't let your food get cold. Eat."

AFTER DINNER, as we'd walked through Times Square, our arms locked together, Dario had whispered up into my ear, "I want to go back to your place with you."

I'd practically tripped over my own feet when he'd said that, but I'd managed to nod my head like I was comfortable with it. And so there we were.

Dario lay on one of the double beds, his arms beneath his head, just looking at me as I stood there with a cold can of Sprite in each hand. I placed them on the nightstand between the beds, and then I just stood there some more, not sure if I should lie down beside him or if I should go get on the other bed. But he slid over and patted the place on the bed next to him, which gave me a strong clue as to what he expected. So I stretched out beside him.

He reached right down to my waist and grabbed the hem of my polo shirt, pulling it up over my head with a single whooshing movement. Then he drew back to look at me. My instinct was to hide myself. I tried to cover my chest by crossing my arms, but he pushed them gently to my sides, and then continued to take in the sight of my bare chest.

"You are just the way I imagined you would be."

I wondered what he meant by that. After all, I was quite toned from my time on the fishing boat but definitely not exactly chiseled, slightly tanned but not a beautiful shade of brown, covered by a sprinkling of chest hair, not hairless and marble-smooth. Although men and women often stared at me, apparently intrigued by my appearance, I'd never considered myself drop-dead gorgeous in a pretty way, and I wasn't a supermanly hairy bear.

And add to that knowledge, the way he was looking at me…. With Dario studying me like that, I couldn't think straight enough to come up with a thing to say. Not exactly surprising, I guess, knowing me. But Dario didn't seem to have talking on his mind, anyways. He lunged onto my chest, and his lips went to work, kissing and sucking and nibbling at my skin. The way he touched me was inspired, maybe even frenzied, and it felt good. And, yeah, I was just as horny as the next guy, but fooling around was just so different when I actually *knew* the guy I was with. Doing this with Dario was *nothing* like fooling around with some dude I didn't know, and didn't care to get to know, and that fact was basically blowing my mind. After a couple of minutes, I found myself curling up into a ball.

At first, Dario didn't seem even slightly fazed by the way I curled up. After all, I'd been holding back from him since day one, and he was accustomed to my attempts at hiding. "Philippe, I want you, and… I'll take any part of you that you are willing to give me." He was soon pushing my legs down, trying to uncurl my body.

I lifted up my head and tried to look into his eyes. "I'm not used to this."

But he pressed on, like I hadn't said anything, his hands now moving to the sides of my face and clutching there, to hold my head still. "I do not mean to push you… but just let me kiss you…." His breathed the words against my cheek, and I noticed that his exhales were coming out in tightly controlled heaves. But then, so were mine. "You are so sweet to me… never met someone like you…."

I was incredibly turned on by this combined physical and verbal assault, and all signs pointed to him feeling very much the same way, but this was happening so quickly—*too* quickly for me. At this point, Dario had somehow managed to flatten my body under his on the bed and was again on top of my chest, now kissing my lips with an open mouth as he ground his hips against mine. Even through our shorts, I could feel his hard-on pressing into mine.

I was starting to lose it. His need and my need, well, added up together, the emotional pressure was just too much for me to handle. Because I knew that Dario wanted *me* and not just my body, which might sound like a positive thing, but for me, it was just too complicated. And I wasn't ready for it.

"Let's go slower… please slow down, Dario."

Finally, my words seemed to sink in and he yanked himself off my chest and then flopped back flat beside me on the bed. "I'm sorry. Philippe… I'm sorry. I guess I sort of… attacked you, didn't I?" His chest was rising and falling quickly, like he'd been dancing hard for an hour straight. He looked toward the window and took a single deep breath. "It seems I have gotten carried away."

I felt guilty, and I didn't know just why. "I'm the one who should be sorry, Dario… I'm really into you, but… I'm just… this feels like a lot all at once."

He sat up and pulled me beside him so that we were both sitting and looking into each other's eyes. The skin all around his eyes was dark right now, shadowed even, and I knew that I was the cause of the troubles that made him look this way.

"No, don't apologize. I think I am starting to understand why I want to be with you so much. It's just, Philippe, you are so *different* from the other men I have known."

"Different? I'm *different*?" That didn't sound much like a compliment, not that I particularly enjoyed those.

"Oh, yes, so different… and truthfully, I want you so much more. There is something addictive about you. You are so soft and pretty, but masculine, too. And I just want to taste you and to touch you, and get my fill of you, but—" He smiled rather sheepishly. "—I suppose I cannot do it all at once… at least, I cannot do it all tonight." Dario stretched out flat on his back with his eyes closed and his forearm draped across his face. He sighed, and said, "It's fine… we do *not* have to do anything else physically, but I really want to stay with you tonight."

I knew I had to touch him, just so he'd know that he moved my heart in the same way that I moved his. And since words were not my forte, I could think of only one way to let him know how much I cared. So I leaned down and slowly began to unbutton his shirt, because, like I'd promised him, I was going to take a chance. It just couldn't happen in a frenzied rush.

"I want to feel your skin against mine, Dario... but we need to go *slowly*."

He watched with wide unsure eyes as I undid his buttons. After all, I *had* just shut him down in a major way.

No wonder he's confused.

Once all of the buttons were undone, he raised himself just enough to allow me to pull his shirt from off his shoulders, but he still looked puzzled. I took a few long seconds to run my fingertips, back and forth, over his smooth chest, causing his nipples to perk up with interest. In my opinion, Dario was perfect, sweet as candy to my hands as much as to my eyes. I shifted so I was lying back flat on the bed beside him, and I gently pulled the entirety of his slim frame over on top of me (he'd seemed to like it up there) so that our chests were pressed together, our hard dicks lined up through our shorts.

I didn't grind my hips against his, even though I wanted to badly. He was not one of those no-name dudes from my time in Gloucester, and I wouldn't treat him as if he was. So instead, I put my hands on either side of his face, and I drew him down into a kiss as I had never done to my anonymous partners. With that first closed-mouth kiss, I thanked him chastely for all of the care and attention and patience he'd showed to both Sophie and me since we'd come to New York City. I took a shallow breath, and with the next kiss, I used the tip of my tongue to part his lips in an effort to show him how much I wanted him, even though I wasn't ready for all of him tonight. And in my next kiss, which, at this point, had escalated into a fevered coupling of our tongues, together inside his mouth, I let him know how much I admired him as a person and as an artist. Somehow, I was pretty sure he understood everything I was trying to express.

I could tell from the way he struggled to hold himself back that Dario was used to being in charge and that he *liked* to be in control, especially in bed. But nonetheless, he allowed me to set tonight's pace because he knew I needed to. Although I went on to kiss him many more times, gradually the heat between us cooled, as we both knew that they were not intended to lead us to increased intimacy. Each kiss became more leisurely than the next. At some point, I actually lost track of where we were and how we got there, but I kissed him until we were starting to fall asleep, our lips still pressed together. But just before we dropped off, I felt Dario move away from me, and soon he was tugging down my pants and then his own. Instinctively, I knew it was not so we could do anything more sexually but just so we could be comfortable. I slept in my baggy flannel boxers, he in his tight black briefs, our bare legs wrapped up together.

For the first time, I slept in the safety of a caring man's arms.

I didn't need to hide because I knew was safe there.

I WOKE up to the sight of Dario's dark eyes; his intense gaze was all I could see. Better even than waking up to the sun rising over the water on the wide Atlantic. And by his pensive expression, I could tell he'd been doing some thinking.

It was as if he'd been waiting for me to wake up. "I have a question for you, Philippe."

He always wanted to know more and more about me, which made hiding incredibly difficult. I shrugged in response.

"You are a virgin, aren't you?"

The man was nothing if not direct. "That sounds more like an accusation."

How does he know every personal detail about me?

"You didn't get busy with me last night when I could tell your *body* wanted to as badly as mine did."

I pulled away from him. "So what if I *am* a virgin?"

"What if *I am not?*" For a split second, I saw worry in his eyes.

"Well, *maybe* I've been *close* to some guys, but just not... not full-out sex."

"*Maybe* I am not even *close* to being a virgin." I saw more concern; it was written on his whole face now.

I took his hand from where it rested on my chest and squeezed it hard. Actions were so much easier for me than words. "*Maybe* it doesn't matter what we did before we met each other. Because *maybe* all that matters is what happens between us now."

"*Maybe* I want to be the only guy you see."

"*Maybe* I had no plans to see any guy but you." He reached around me, and I was pulled roughly against his chest.

"*Maybe*, just *maybe*, you made me the happiest man in Manhattan this morning." I felt his arms tighten their hold on me until it almost hurt.

"*Maybe* the feeling is mutual."

I had no clue how, but I'd found the first place that I'd ever fit just perfectly: in Dario Pereira's arms.

15

I DON'T know exactly when it happened. I mean, I can't really pinpoint a specific moment or even the day things changed, but it seemed like somewhere along the line Dario and I had become a solid couple. Before he left that Sunday morning, after I'd slept so well in his arms for the first time, he had picked up my cell phone from the bureau and programmed his number into it without bothering to ask for my permission. I didn't need to return the favor as Henri had given him my number ages ago.

"I expect you to use it." He'd then placed the phone back down on the bureau and looked at me in his direct way—a way that made me feel as naked as I did in some of my nightmares. His direct order had startled me a bit, I'll admit, but I'd swallowed hard and nodded anyways. I was becoming as accustomed to his demands as he was to my attempts to conceal myself.

So that morning, after getting a quick just-checking-in phone call from my "boyfriend," Sophie and I headed off to visit Marymount Manhattan College. Since school was out for the summer, there were no regular dance classes for us to observe, so Sophie and I just took a general college tour. Many of the school buildings were a traditional brick and more than respectably constructed. There was also that artsy feeling that I knew Sophie liked, maybe not as intense as it had been at SUNY Purchase, but it was there, and how can you complain about the campus? It's New York City! And like at SUNY Purchase, I had to fight off the images of myself as a student here that kept flashing in my mind.

On our trip back to Steps on Broadway where Sophie was planning to take an afternoon ballet class with a new-to-her teacher, we sat next to each other on the subway, our knees banging against each other's.

I dared to ask, "Did you like Marymount Manhattan?"

And for once she didn't hesitate. "I liked it a lot, especially that it's right in Manhattan, but I feel like I'm at a loss to make a judgment about it because I wasn't able to observe ballet and modern classes. I think I'm gonna talk to Dario about it and see what he thinks."

Sophie trusted Dario. Maybe someday I would trust myself enough to be able to fully trust him too.

Maybe that day is coming closer.

But to be honest, I didn't *want* to trust Dario fully—not just yet. Being in a relationship was still so new to me. I'd always tried my hardest to avoid getting into situations where I had to be accountable, and for so long, I'd *refused* to put myself in a place where I would have to live up to another person's emotional expectations of me. Ever since I'd lost Mom, I'd been very much a loner. And not just because that was how I'd wanted it, which, in fact, it was, but also because I'd *needed* to be an island. Dependent on no one. I couldn't let myself be hurt again as I had when Mom had been torn away from me, and I'd still needed her so much. I'd always figured that devastating pain like that couldn't possibly happen to loners.

And another rule of thumb I'd long kept in mind: making yourself visible to someone—putting yourself on his radar—*that* was what set you up for a fall. And I'd long refused to be scrutinized the way a boyfriend might do. After all, I was one to hide, not to display myself.

What have I gotten myself into?

"You have the strangest look on your face, Phil. What are you thinking about?"

I looked over at Sophie, shocked that she had come to know me well enough to recognize on my face the signs that my mind was running away with its concerns. "It's nothing for you to worry about." I heard the ugly ring of patronization in my own voice.

And then Sophie did the strangest thing: she reached over, lifted my palm off the strap of my backpack that leaned between my legs, and pulled my hand onto her knee.

Still studying my eyes with her pale blue ones, she said, "We're family, Uncle Phil. I'll always worry about you, just like you'll always worry about me. There's no way around it."

I can handle this moment. I can, I told myself out of pure habit.

I sucked in a deep, steadying breath.

Maybe I actually can....

I made an effort to grin at her, but I had a feeling it seemed fake. "Of course we worry about each other, kid. It's part of the whole family deal. But this is *personal*, and—"

"And you don't want to let me in on your *personal* life?" Those light eyes flooded with tears. Tears I doubted she'd allow herself to shed because of her reserved sense of pride.

I shook my head, scratched my beard, and then I shrugged and possibly sniffed a few times, for good measure. At this point, though, I hadn't come up with a plan for how to respond, because Sophie's words had hit the nail on the head.

"It's okay. I know *how you are*. I just thought we'd gotten past all that, having spent so much time together this summer, and all."

I could only open up so much for my own emotional safety, but because I truly loved Sophie and would not see her feelings hurt by my senseless hang-ups, I answered. "Maybe I was thinking about Dario."

In response, Sophie smiled, her expression suddenly smug. "That's what I figured." And when she squeezed my hand, she added, "You guys are totally boyfriends now, aren't you?"

"It is starting to look that way." I managed a more genuine smile than my last one, and then, of course, I blushed. "It's hard for me to… uh, to *do this* with him." My eyes tracked an empty water bottle that was rolling around haphazardly on the subway car's floor.

"Dario's very special. I think he's good for you."

"But I don't know if I can be *somebody's*, Sophie… in that way."

"Well, I think you can do it. I mean, you're doing an excellent job of being *mine* this summer. *My* tour guide, *my* chaperone… *my* friend."

I can handle loving Sophie this much… I can.

Thankfully, the train stopped right then, and we had to get out. I stood up quickly and turned toward the doors, but Sophie didn't let go of my hand. She tugged on it a bit, clearly having something else to say. "It'll work out, if you stop running and just let things with Dario happen."

I was fairly sure that my niece was right. Again.

16

THAT NIGHT, Dario was showcasing the work of one of the dance teachers who he substitute-taught for at Broadway Dance Center. I sat in the small black box theater beside Sophie, Emily, Sara, and a girl named Linny I'd met only a couple of times before. All the lights were turned down, and it was silent. As excited as I was to see him perform, though, I was also dreading it at the same time. I knew that when Dario performed, he would be placing his heart out there on display for the world to see, and I had come to understand how difficult that was for him to do, which made me worry *for* him. I also knew that I was afraid for Dario to bare his soul to *me*, and that's exactly what he'd be doing, even if we were in a crowded room filled with strangers. The biggest problem being, the very same soul baring might be expected of me in return.

And there was one more cause for concern that I should mention. And I knew this as well as I knew my own mother's name: when I witnessed the full physical and emotional splendor of his performance, I would fall more deeply in love with Dario Pereira than I already was.

Yes. That's what I said. *In love.*

The music started, eerie high-pitched, wailing strings of a lone violin, coming together erratically, ensnaring me in a web of uneasiness. Two dancers stepped out onto the floor. Both were male, each swaddled across the middle by only a small swath of black fabric. The tension in their tightened muscles as they posed, ready to burst into action, was almost hard to look at. Then they began to move.

The two men, Dario and an African-American man just a bit smaller but every bit as strong, wove in and out of one another's bodies, reminding me of the wind blowing through laundry as it hung lifelessly on a clothesline. The wind, or Dario, made the laundry, the black man, move in ways that were so peculiar that they *had* to come directly from Mother herself—no ordinary human being could have come up with those odd combinations of twists and turns. Then with an eruption of energy, the laundry seemed to come alive, suddenly possessing a power all its own, and it shaped the wind with its newly found strength.

The expression on Dario's dusky face, which never fully emerged from the shadowy lighting, shifted from commanding to submissive and then slid into something sort of blissful. I couldn't say if his partner's face mirrored these expressions as I was too captivated by Dario's every movement to notice anything else in the room. Dario's motions were at first sure and controlling, his strength and power brimming to the surface, only to later fall prey to the dominance of the other dancer; he cringed and hunched as he sank to the floor. And I wanted to go to him and boost him up, to comfort him, so that he'd dance again.

There was a story to the dance, one that I either recognized or imagined, a tale of love's constantly changing hold on a couple's united soul, in which each partner experienced moments of glory as well as moments of suffering at the hands of the other. This rising and falling of pain and joy seemed as natural as the wind blowing through the folds of a cotton shirt hanging on a backyard clothesline to dry.

By the end of the number, I was spent. Through Dario and his partner's movements, I had somehow experienced the anguish and the joy of two lovers as they learned each other's ways. Even at intermission, I had trouble making small talk with Sophie and her friends. I hadn't been the one to dance, but still I was drained, and the only thing that could fill me back up was five solid minutes in Dario's arms.

After the show, our small crowd waited outside on the street for Dario to emerge from the backstage door.

"Phil, Linny lives right near Peridance in Union Square, and she wants us all to stay over her house tonight, then we can go to ballet class together tomorrow morning. Is that okay?"

I turned to Sophie and stared. I'd forgotten that she was even with me. "Huh?" It was a good thing she was seventeen, and not seven.

"*Uncle Phil*, wake up and smell the coffee, would you? Linny Goldstein takes the same ballet class as me, Sara, and Em at Peridance. You've met her mom like five times... you know, Thelma. Remember?"

An image of a smiling face perched beside mine, our noses pressed against the glass as we peered through the window into the ballet studio in an effort to catch a glimpse of the girls as they moved across the dance floor. "Oh, yeah... I remember her."

"Can I sleep over at her house tonight, and then all four of us will go to ballet together in the morning?"

"Well, sure, but don't you need to get stuff from the hotel? A leotard and tights and...."

Sophie pointed to the dance bag that hung from her shoulder. "We just came from ballet class. We're gonna wear yesterday's stuff."

Emily pinched the tip of her nose. "Just call us the stinky ballerinas."

"The teacher won't need to see us coming; he'll be able to *smell* us!"

I looked at Sophie, standing in the middle of this small group of girls, making jokes and laughing, appearing more normal than I'd ever thought possible. I smiled at that. "Of course, you can go. I'll meet you over at Peridance tomorrow. Just call me to let me know when."

Just then Dario pushed through the backstage door, and the girls clustered around him like groupies. "This is Dario Pereira. He's choreographing my college audition solo." Sophie's voice rang out loud and clear, and very proud of her teacher. "And he teaches lots of professional classes around the city."

For a moment, Dario disappeared in a pile of hugging arms and squeals of girlish chatter. When he popped out of the pile, he was a bit flustered and pink-cheeked, but really happy. We said goodbye to the girls and headed down the street toward the subway.

IT WAS as if I was attuned to Dario's body in a different way since I'd seen him perform that night. I mean, I started to notice all of these tiny things—meaningless things, really—in the way he moved himself from place A to place B. In how he stepped into the subway like he owned it... in how he tossed his loose black bangs sideways off of his forehead with a thrust of a single shoulder... in how he hovered close beside me at all times.

"Want to get something to eat?" He turned to me, his perfect features wrinkled quizzically in an effort to read my mood.

But I could only stare at his mouth as he spoke.

"Backstage, somebody delivered a huge fruit basket to us. So I don't need food right now, if you don't."

I nodded, and then I shook my head.

"Are you okay, Philippe? You are acting sort of strange."

"You were amazing." The words fell out of my mouth.

Dario smiled just enough that I knew he was pleased. "You liked it?"

I nodded again. "Um, Dario, please… come back to my hotel… with me… right now."

When Dario stopped short to gawk at me, the guy walking behind him on the sidewalk literally crashed into his backside. "Oh, sorry," Dario said as the guy sent him a "get with the program" glance and stepped around us.

"Come back to my room…. I want to… to be…." Dario seemed to get the picture, although I'm not exactly sure how.

"You don't have to ask me three times." He grabbed my hand, stepped to the edge of the street, and flagged down a cab.

WE WERE side-by-side, sprawled flat out on the double bed closest to my hotel room's big window. The lights were off, but there was enough of a glow from the New York City night filtering in through the filmy curtain that we could see each other.

Dario turned onto his side. "It has barely been a week since you asked me to slow down in the bedroom, and I find myself here again… and by your invitation."

I felt heat rise to my cheeks; what he said was nothing short of the truth. I'd certainly given him mixed messages.

"And after some serious thought this past week, I have decided that there is no real rush for us to be intimate." He was studying my face. "You are worth waiting for, Philippe, so…."

I searched my mind for the reason that in the space of just one week I was certain that I ready for more with Dario, but I came up empty. "I… I just… am." I covered my face with my hands. "Ready, that is."

"Come here, let me hold you."

Obediently, I turned onto my side and backed right up against him, snuggling up to his chest. The hardness of his dick pressed against my lower back as he wrapped his arms around my shoulders.

"You are something of an enigma to me, do you know that?"

I shrugged, and then felt the underside of his chin pressing steadily on my shoulder, pushing it back down where it belonged. "I think... I'm changing a lot, Dario. *A lot*... and really fast... inside my head, you know?" That was the best I could do, in terms of an explanation for my behavior.

It was as if Dario could sense that words alone weren't moving us forward in the way we needed. He pushed me onto my back rather forcefully and leaned over me to look at my face. His eyes were darker than the deepest parts of the ocean, where its floor was miles beneath the water's surface. And in the same way that the deepest parts of the ocean were threatening, so, too, was the expression in Dario's eyes. Because I knew that he saw me—*he really saw me*—in a way no one else had for a very long time. I supposed that since my mother's death, I hadn't let anyone close enough to get a good look at the parts of my soul that you could only see by staring into my eyes, just the way Dario was doing right now.

His desire for me was evident in his inquisitive expression, in his rapid breathing, and in the way he held me—and since *I* had brought him to my bed because I'd wanted this closeness with him, I planned to own up to my own desires. In fact, I *wanted* to own up physically to the feelings I had developed for him. So when Dario shifted his chest so it was fully centered on mine, I allowed myself to relax; his weight felt comforting on top of me. And when his lips finally met mine, I was ready for the spark and the flame and the burn that I'd never experienced in those hookups back in Gloucester.

I wasn't sure how, but Dario seemed to know that I needed an anchor—something to hold me down during our ensuing lovemaking—to keep me from drifting away. He took one of my wrists solidly in his grasp, and by doing so, he secured me to him. While kissing me, he slid to my side and somehow managed to remove my clothes and toss them into a neat pile on the floor beside the bed; I hadn't even realized I was being undressed. And then just as efficiently, he took off his own clothes. When we were both naked, he climbed back on top of me, making me feel like I was surrounded by warm, brown skin.

I was inexperienced with this kind of tenderness, but Dario clearly was not. And as a lover, he moved in much the same way that he did as a dancer. Sure of hand, powerful in his attack, but willing to be touched and molded when the moment called for it. Dario rubbed his smooth chest rather exotically against mine, and soon he was making a similar motion with the sharp bones of his hips, his erection between them, impossible for me to overlook. As he ground his hips against mine, I realized that it was in no way a frenzied humping, which was all I'd ever known of sex until that very moment. He moved with purpose, rotating in predictable circles of pleasure that I found my own hips waiting for and rising to meet.

It seemed Dario had brought along in his backpack condoms and lube, as they magically appeared on the nightstand, and soon I found myself being prepared for what would come next. Always so closed to new people and to new experiences, I found myself being opened in a way I'd never known. Within minutes, Dario had opened my body up to the point that I was trembling.

And then abruptly, he stopped his preparation of my body. "Do you want this?" After asking so directly, he waited without a word for my answer. I somehow knew he would not proceed until he heard me say yes.

I took a minute to think about my answer. As it was my first time being truly intimate, I admittedly felt awkward and wasn't sure of what to expect. But I knew that I was ready and… I knew that I wanted this.

That I want him.

I nodded and admitted the truth. "I want you."

And then Dario slowly, but purposefully, made his way inside my body; once he began his trek, he never hedged. Surely, I felt a lot of pressure during his gradual entry, but it wasn't really what I'd call pain. What was harder for me to deal with than the physical part of Dario's entry into me, though, was that I sensed the blossoming of a new emotional connection between us. Looking down at me, Dario's gaze was gentle, and combined with the way his lips curved upward softly, I couldn't help but suspect that he really cared for me. I'd never been looked at like this before—that much, I could say for certain. And I knew that he saw every facet of emotion in my eyes, as there was nowhere to hide my own gaze except inside of his.

As I adjusted to the feeling of him moving inside me, the pleasure became more and more intense, but I remained aware that it was secondary to the intensity of the emotional bond that we were forging. I was closer to Dario than I had ever been to anyone, even to my very own mother—an intimacy I had thought lost to me forever. Soon, though, I couldn't disregard the pleasure any longer. It was dragging me out to rougher waters, where I had to leave all awareness of myself—of being lost, of being seen, of being scared—behind. It was as if Dario and I were floating together on the roiling ocean, and I was now tethered to him by the steadily moving grip of his hand on my dick.

Before my brain even had a chance to give it the "go ahead," I started to climax in a manner so devastating that I'll admit I never even imagined it could happen like that. As I struggled to stay in one piece, I saw in Dario's eyes the very same struggle, and then I heard a low moan that could only come from sexual release. I wasn't sure if I was the one who'd made that sound or if it had been my lover. I guess it really didn't matter.

SHE WAS wasting away... right before my eyes. There was nothing I could do to stop it. Whatever part of her body that I grabbed, well... well, it just disintegrated into black sooty dust between my fingers. First her hands... and then her arms. The side of her face crumbled away next... and I wasn't ready for her to be gone... not now... not yet. And when the wind came and blew so fiercely, I knew she wasn't coming back... she was gone for good now. Because her dusty ashes—all that was left of her—rose up in the breeze. And I swore that inside the swirl of those ashes I saw Dario's face... and then his whole body... leaping and turning like he was dancing. So I scrambled around... trying to catch them both... to hold onto them... to keep them with me... but they whirled right through my fingers.

"Mom!" I shouted *her* name, but it was an image of Dario's eyes I saw in the dark. And through the haze of sleep, I heard the panic in my own voice; it was loud enough to wake me. It woke Dario too.

"Hey, Philippe... wake up. I want you to wake up right now."

In a very small voice, I replied to him. "I'm awake." I'd been having one of my feelings dreams. And in the final stage of my feelings dreams, I always reached for my fading mother. That part never failed to wake me up, or maybe I should say jolt me into consciousness.

The night before, I'd taken a step forward by trusting Dario enough to make love to him.

Why do I have to take two steps backward with a dream like this?

"Are you okay? I think you might have been dreaming."

"I... I-I dream sometimes."

"Tell me about it... *please, Philippe.*" And yes, it was one of those commanding sorts of "pleases," but even more insistent than usual, like he somehow knew that understanding my dream was important to knowing exactly who I was.

"I'm sorry... I don't like to talk about it." *Especially when it's more about you than it is about my mother right now.*

"You are my lover. You need to tell me what scares you."

What scares me.... What is it that scares me?

"*You* scare me, Dario.... Loving you scares me." That summed up the problem fairly well.

"And do you love me, Philippe?"

"I'm trying very hard not to."

17

"I THINK that Tisch School of the Arts at NYU is just too academic for me."

"So you don't want to even visit? Because you might have to *study too much* if you went there?" We sat downstairs in the Holiday Inn's restaurant, drinking coffee and restructuring the game plan for our dance exploration of New York City in order to make the best use of the time we had left. We would only be here in New York City for three more weeks so we had to figure out which schools we still needed to visit and which modern classes Sophie had yet to try.

"I want to *dance*, Uncle Phil. Yeah, I know I need a degree, but I want to be a dancer, not a college professor."

"If you get hurt, though, it's good to have a degree to fall back on." I sounded like somebody's father.

"*You're* injured—what do *you* have to fall back on?"

That snarky girl was back. *What happened to the sweet Sophie?* "I have absolutely *nothing* to fall back on—and that's my point. I have no clue what I'm going to do with my life next." Saying it out loud made it real. I felt goose bumps rise on my arms, a reaction to stark fear, most likely.

But my words had the desired effect. "Oh, all right. I guess I see what you're saying." She sighed loudly in resignation.

"So we need to really focus on our goals right up until we have to leave. What's on the day plan?"

"Well, I'm going to look at Juilliard with my friends. Not that I'd ever get in there, but going with the girls seems less scary somehow than making an official visit with your uncle."

I didn't feel like the most "official" person in the world, and I hardly felt like an uncle, for that matter, but I knew what she was getting at. "You have as much of a chance to get in there as anyone else does, kid."

She shrugged. "*Whatever, Uncle*.... I don't know if I'm up for the 'Juilliard' kind of pressure, that's all. And I really liked SUNY Purchase, which is almost as hard to get into, so, anyways, *what's your point*?"

I took a breath before I answered, refusing to allow Sophie's insecurities to alter our game plan. "What do you need from me *today*, Soph? Remember, I'm here to help you."

It was as if she stumbled into the realization that she'd gone just a bit over the top in the teenage-brat direction. "Sorry for being bitchy. I guess looking at schools is a lot of pressure, that's all."

I nodded at her, fully understanding the pressure of trying to make plans, which I hadn't yet had the courage to do, and took my last bite of eggs.

"I'm so psyched, though, 'cause Dario and me are gonna finish up the choreography for my solo tonight. So how about if I meet you for dinner at the Così near Peridance and we go to my lesson together from there?"

"Where are you going to take ballet class?"

"I'll take ballet at Peridance, then meet you right after."

"You don't want me to meet you at Juilliard and take you over to Peridance for ballet?"

"I'm *totally* capable of getting there with my friends, or, for that matter, *by myself*... uh, not to be nasty or anything."

"You're starting to know this city like the back of your hand, aren't you?"

She smiled, and I could tell it came from her heart. "New York City's like a home away from home. I really like it here."

Sophie was looking at me as if she was expecting me to gush on and on about how much I loved the city too, but I refused to fall into that trap. Because I *was* afraid that I *was* starting to like this city just a bit too much for my own good. I just had to keep reminding myself, as Sophie should, that since people couldn't be permanent fixtures in our lives, neither could places. I couldn't afford to let myself get carried away with this romantic summer in NYC.

People and places, they come and go in your life like the wind through laundry hanging on a line. Right now, they are here... and then, they'll be there... but soon enough, all is still.

You find yourself alone... and not by your own choice.

DARIO AND I decided to meet at the Così for a cup of tea before dinner. Sometimes he liked to meet at a restaurant simply to talk, not just to eat.

"You should have seen these little kids I taught in my boys' ballet class today, Phil. They were so adorable."

"At the New Jersey studio?"

"Yeah... I really like teaching there. They appreciate me a lot, especially the mothers."

"That's because you look really good in tights." *He really does.*

Dario laughed, and it was such a clean, pure sound that I wanted to bottle it up so I could listen to it again later when I was alone. "And *that* is not what I meant... but thanks. What I was trying to say is that the mothers are just so glad that their sons have an adult male dancer to be a role model. Most ballet classes are taught by women."

That made sense. "I think I know what you mean. I actually have been hanging out a lot with this little boy at the Holiday Inn's pool. His mom is in the middle of a nasty divorce, and she's usually trying to make phone calls or something, you know, trying to get her life back together. So the boy and I swim with each other. I think he likes having another guy around because his dad travels a lot."

"That is really sweet, Philippe. And he is a lucky guy if he gets to have you in a Speedo, all to himself!"

"The boy is *four*... and I wear shorts, not bikini bottoms, dude." I slugged him playfully on his shoulder, and he winked at me. That's when it hit me that I felt comfortable—*completely* comfortable—in Dario's presence.

Dario pulled his chair closer to mine. "So tell me, Phil, when is your niece going to another sleepover party? I am finding it hard to sleep without you night after night."

Trying to hide that little strip of my reddened cheeks that I bet he could see between my hair and beard, I leaned closer to him. "Yeah, me too."

"Maybe when Sophie goes back to Massachusetts, you could come stay with me at my place for a while?" Dario looked down at his hands, which were both wrapped too tightly around his mug. It seemed that he knew me well enough to be unsure as to what my reaction to his suggestion would be. "So what do you say?"

My brain scrambled wildly for an answer, and once I found it, I then had to rush to find the right words to express it. "Sometimes, Dario… it's like sometimes I worry that this isn't real, you know, things between you and me. And I try not to think about you… and future times with you… too much, because… sometimes I think that the next time I look for you, you're gonna be gone."

That really isn't much of an answer, is it?

But it appeared that Dario also knew me well enough not to be overly shocked or hurt by my words. He looked up at me and shook his head slowly, but his voice was still tough. "You are going to figure it out eventually, Bergeron—I am not going anywhere. I have looked around, and I've never before seen a guy like you. Somebody who's *real*…. Someone who's honest enough to admit that he's trying not to love me."

I looked at him squarely. "And I'm *still* trying."

"I hope you fail miserably in that endeavor." I then got the sexiest kiss that Dario could get away with in a family restaurant.

18

IT LOOKED like Dario was going to get his wish for a sleepover that weekend. Henri had decided to come to the city from Friday night until Sunday to visit with Sophie and get a sneak preview of her college audition solo. And since Henri wasn't a Holiday Inn type of guy, he'd made other, more exclusive, arrangements: something with Trump in its name, a full-size suite for Soph and him, and a floor-to-ceiling view of Central Park.

He'd left it up to Sophie to pick a place where we would have dinner when he got there on Friday night. Since the two of them were crazy about Tom Hanks and made a point of seeing all of his movies together, Sophie thought it would be fun to eat dinner at Bubba Gump Shrimp, and then the three of us could walk around Times Square together to give Henri, as she said, "a chance to take a bite of The Big Apple."

Sophie had a late afternoon private lesson with Dario, so Henri had checked into his suite and was meeting us at the restaurant. Before we found Henri, who had texted that he was seated upstairs waiting for us, we stopped by the restaurant's gift shop where Sophie picked up three Bubba Gump Shrimp Co. baseball caps, one for each of us.

She then informed me that we were all going to wear them when we walked around Times Square after dinner. "You know Dad, he'll *love* the whole matching hats thing!"

I was extremely surprised, and equally impressed, that Sophie would be willing to do something like that for her father. I guessed her action showed that Sophie was growing up and becoming more able to put other people's needs before her own. And she was right—Henri loved goofy stuff like wearing matching "Run Forrest Run" hats!

Henri was waiting at a table by the window that overlooked Broadway. When he saw us, he stood up, an ear-to-ear grin spread across his face, and he reached for Sophie. "Oh, God, Soph, I've missed you!" He squeezed her shoulders hard, his brawny frame curving in all around her, and after pushing her back a step or two so he could look her up and down, he pulled her in for yet another bear hug. "Jesus, it's good to see you, little girl!" Where I was quiet and withdrawn, Henri was my polar opposite. He was outgoing, vociferous, and maybe even a little bit flashy. Still holding onto Sophie with one arm, he looked over at me.

I stuck out my hand to shake, but he was having none of that. "Group hug!" he called out, and I was pulled into the mix.

"Okay, okay... Henri, let's sit down."

Sophie nodded at me in embarrassed agreement. "Yeah, Dad. I'm thirsty... I want to order some lemonade."

As we sat down, her father informed her that he'd already ordered her one, and that it was going to come with some kind of light bulb/ice cube thing floating in it. "Thanks, Dad...." and then I heard her mumble under her breath, "but *hello*, I'm almost eighteen."

"So, family—I want to hear *every* detail of your time here in The Big Apple. Who's gonna start?"

Very predictably, I looked at Sophie to begin, and she looked at me for the same reason. "He's *your* father, kid."

So Sophie launched into her description of each of the schools and dance programs we'd visited together. Finally, she described The Juilliard School, from when she'd checked it out with her friends, and then provided her rationale for why she didn't want to apply to NYU's Tisch School of the Arts.

"I'm not sure I agree with that decision, Sophie." Henri grimaced and then looked over at me as if he was irritated that I'd let Sophie stray from the official plans. "I thought we'd decided that NYU was on our list, Philippe."

"It was a tentative list, Henri, and it's *her* college list, not *ours*."

"Nonetheless, I think that Sophie and I will take a walk around NYU for an informal visit tomorrow."

Sophie rolled her eyes. "Whatever."

Henri, have you met the snarky side of Sophie?

Henri's head pivoted toward Sophie, a bit surprised by her attitude, and then he laughed heartily. "'*Whatever*'? I'll be paying for your education, young lady, so I think I should have at least a little bit of input." Then he shifted his attention back to me again. "So how's your love life?"

I sent Sophie a condemning glare, knowing she must have spilled the beans about Dario and me, and she very appropriately blushed and looked down at the floor beside her chair. "It's just fine; thanks for asking." Enough said in my opinion, but I knew that Henri would want more.

"So tell me about this Dario Pereira...." He looked back and forth from Sophie to me. "Somebody had better start talking."

"He's an awesome teacher, Dad. He's changed my entire posture, especially the way I hold my hips in ballet."

The waitress approached our table, and as expected, Henri ordered for all of us. "We'll start with a couple orders of popcorn shrimp and all of the different dipping sauces... it's what you're famous for, right, young lady?"

The waitress smiled. "That's for sure, sir. Our shrimp is the best."

He brushed back his short light-brown bangs from where they drooped on his forehead. "And we'll all share an order of Dumb Luck Coconut Shrimp, Forrest's Seafood Feast, and a Dixie Style Baby Back Ribs. Bring as many different sides as we can get with these meals, I'm gonna leave the details about that up to you, and another beer and an iced tea." He tapped his finger on the rim of his empty glass.

"And a house salad," Sophie piped up.

Henri sent her a that-better-not-be-all-you're-planning-to-eat look, and Sophie said, "Don't have a cow, Dad... I'm gonna try a little bit of everything. Not that I need an excuse, but I just happen to *like* salad."

After the waitress headed off, Henri's one-track mind found its way back to the subject of Dario. "And Philippe, have you had a chance to spend much time with the man?"

I was quite skilled at avoiding topics that I was uncomfortable discussing, which, unfortunately for me, wasn't a particularly narrow field. "Well, Sophie takes three lessons from him every week, so *we* see him regularly."

"Hmpf." Henri gulped down a quarter of his beer in one big swig. "That's not exactly what I was asking you."

"Dario and Philippe are boyfriends. You should see them together, Dad, they are so cute!"

Under the table, I kicked Sophie lightly. Not hard enough to do any damage, but just so I was certain that she felt it.

"Is that so?" Henri put down his glass with a thud. "I am happy to hear it. So, Phil, does that mean you are going to stay in the city? No more fishing boats?"

This was exactly why I hated to talk about things. Both of them were looking at me, wanting answers to questions that I hadn't even allowed myself to consider yet. "I don't know, Henri. I'm just going to see what happens, I guess."

"You, Philippe, have got to *make* things happen. You can't just wait around and see how things unfold. No, you've gotta step up to the plate— take a swing! Don't strike out looking."

Baseball analogies? Those only started up when Henri meant business. "You'll meet him tomorrow. I think you'll like him." I tried to change the subject.

"It isn't about if *I* like him or not—it's about whether *you* like him."

"So, anyways, Henri, we rented a dance studio so that Sophie can show you her solo tomorrow afternoon."

"I guess we'll have to cut our NYU visit short, Dad," Sophie said with no shortage of sarcasm. "*Super unfortunately.*"

"And I think it is time you settled down and started a life *off* the ocean, Philippe. Are you hearing me?"

We were all talking *at* each other now, which was so typical of our family. As I sucked down my iced tea, I repeated "Lalalalala" in my head, which helped to block out Henri's speech.

Sophie whined, "Dad, I have to *like* the college I go to. And I've seen some I like, but I'm *really* not into NYU...."

And Henri jabbered on, "Philippe, you are twenty years old, and you need a plan. I was about to enter my junior year of college when I was your age—and I was fully invested in my business degree."

Lalalalala....

We were really quite dysfunctional, but then, this *was* my family. So I took a deep breath and waited for the food to arrive.

AFTER WALKING around Times Square for an hour or so, decked out in our embarrassing Bubba Gump hats, Sophie grabbed her dance bag, which she'd stuffed full with the things she needed for her overnight with Henri, from where it was slung over my shoulder and announced, "Let's go, Dad. I want to check out the Trump International Hotel and Tower. There's a pool, right?"

That was perfectly fine with me. I was more than ready for a break, seeing as Henri wouldn't stop trying to marry me off to Dario to ensure that I'd stay here in the city and I wouldn't ever again set foot on a fishing boat. When I got back to the hotel, Dario was waiting for me in the lobby. And that was *more than* perfectly fine with me. He stood up as soon as he saw me, and I felt a tug at my heart and my groin at the very same time, and I would swear I started to drool a bit, like Pavlov's dog when he saw a bowl of food.

"Nice hat, dude." Dario laughed as he walked over to me with his head upright, his stride smooth and graceful. I knew I had to touch him.

"Uh, it's a family thing." I reached for him. Sometimes I didn't recognize the touchy-feely guy I'd recently turned into... or, at a minimum, who I'd been impersonating so well.

Dario's moved forward. His lips found my ear. "How was dinner? Bubba Gump, right?"

"Bubba Gump was just fine. However, Henri and Sophie were a bit more trying to my patience."

He pulled away from me and sent me a skeptical glance. "At least you have a family to drive you crazy."

I thought for a minute that he was angry, and I briefly wondered how he'd ended up so alone, but then he flashed one of those cool white grins. With relief, I said, "You're right. And believe me, I don't take them for granted." Then I took his hand. "Did you eat dinner?"

"I had yogurt and granola after the class I taught at BDC. I'm hungry for something else.... Famished actually." His expression was nothing if not wolfish.

I felt that heart/groin tug again, but this time it was much more noticeable to me in the groin area. "Have I got anything that might satisfy your appetite upstairs?"

"You have everything I want up there… come on." He took my hand and led me to the elevator.

NOT TO be crude, but I was as hard as a rock by the time I stuck the keycard into the door. I pushed it open, and Dario slammed it behind us. Then I was yanked into his arms.

"You… taste so… damned… good…." Dario somehow managed to say that between making a meal of my lips.

"Unghhh!" I agreed wholeheartedly with his sentiment, but that's what came out.

"I want to taste the rest…." He pushed me backward until I fell onto the bed closest to the door. That's when he made a proper three-course meal of me, starting with my lips and promptly moving south.

Somehow, Dario was able to strip me and kiss me without missing a beat. Our teeth never even banged together once. I lay beneath him, fully naked except for my beard, of course, and strangely, Dario did not seem at all interested in taking off his own clothes. I thought he might have liked the feeling of power he was experiencing from being covered while I was so exposed. He allowed all of his body weight to come down on top of me, driving my back into the soft bed.

And then he opened my mouth with his tongue and grunted against my lips, "Keep your mouth open… and wide."

As I struggled to comply, he dove inside, his tongue reaching and stretching in his effort to learn every corner, every angle, of my mouth. And he swallowed each one of my gasps by sealing his lips tightly over mine. I got light-headed, almost dizzy, really, with the sensation of having my breath stolen away.

Dario's hunger soon shifted its focus onto my beard. He tasted it, his tongue licking and then sucking hard enough that I felt the skin beneath my beard puckering up inside of his mouth. And honestly, I was totally into my passive role—for some reason I didn't understand, or *want* to understand, I craved even more of his control. It just felt right. My chest was the next willing victim to Dario's affectionate assault. He bit down with his front teeth sharply on one of my nipples and then the other, and when I squirmed, he nibbled softly at them, one-by-one, as if he could hardly hold back from making my chest his late-night snack.

"So beautiful, so sweet… Philippe… all I ever wanted… someone like you."

I couldn't form words, as just breathing was proving to be a challenge for me.

But when he moved even lower and his hungry lips began a slow and steady feasting on my dick, another first for me, I was lost. But if I was going to be completely honest, I wasn't lost so much as I was Dario's… even more than I was my own. Whatever he wanted, he only had to ask me and it would be his.

Dario was tireless in his exploration of me. His lips and his teeth and his amazingly talented tongue—not that I had anything to compare it to— devoured my dick, top to bottom and then all of it at once, like I was the only meal he'd ever need.

I writhed beneath him, agonizing in my effort to hold back the inevitable. "I have to come… I wanna do it… please, Dario, say I can.…" I knew that I wasn't making a bit of sense, but at the same time, I knew that he understood my predicament.

He pulled his lips from my dick only long enough to utter, "*I* will tell you when it's time, Philippe… but I'm still hungry for you… not done with you just yet." His breathing was as heavy as mine. "Do not come until I say…"

When I couldn't stand it a second longer, Dario sucked the whole of my dick into his mouth, and then he reached up with both hands and gripped the sides of my face. And then, as my frantic eyes met his greedy ones, he nodded his permission for me to come. So I let myself go completely without removing my gaze from his for a fraction of a second.

I think I love him. Oh, God… I love him.…

Very deliberately, and in no hurry, whatsoever, Dario swallowed, and then he slid his mouth up my length and finally off of my body completely, our stares still locked together. He took a deep breath and then stated with a boldness I envied, "I love you, Philippe. You are *mine,* and I love you."

THAT NIGHT, Dario made love to me over and over again. At first, his loving did nothing short of own me—there was no other way to describe how he took my body as what was rightfully his. As the night wore on, he used his lovemaking like a tool to take me apart, piece-by-piece. Without any mercy, Dario dragged my heart from where it cowered inside my chest, and then he tore my soul from its hiding place, deep inside my heart. When he did those things, he changed me; he changed who I was... what I was made of. And when he fit my pieces back together, I was a different man.

I was now a guy who could say, *and who did say*, "I love you too."

Just before morning had broken, his lovemaking had grown sweet and selfless, and with it, he nurtured me. He was my mother and my father and my lover and my friend. He was the one I could depend on—the one it was okay to need.

And upon my mother's soul, I'd swear this was the whole truth: by the time the morning sunshine had pushed its way through those filmy curtains that shadowed us from the New York City dawn, I wasn't hiding anymore.

I lay spread-eagled on the bed, open to his scrutiny.

I let Dario see all of me.

I don't think I'm even scared at all....

19

WE HAD somehow gathered a small crowd at the little studio that we'd rented so Sophie could show Henri her college audition solo. Dario was there, and I was, too, of course, but my friend Lauren from the hotel pool had also asked if she could come see Sophie dance when I'd mentioned that we were planning the miniperformance for her father. Lauren had Tommy on her lap, and beside her were Sophie's three friends from dance—Emily, Linny, and Sara—all sitting in a single row of metal chairs that Dario and I had set up against the mirror in the front of the studio.

"We have this studio for forty-five more minutes, and that is all. Then some Bollywood group is coming in… and believe me, they will take over. Are you sure your family is going to be here?" Dario seemed a little bit flustered, but I figured maybe he was nervous about his solo being judged live, up close and personal.

I couldn't help it; I touched his cheek to calm him. "Henri and Sophie will be here."

It seemed like my words and my little gesture did the trick, and Dario stopped fretting immediately. "Okay, Philippe, I believe you. Why don't you introduce me to your friend and her little boy?"

I led him over to where Lauren and Tommy sat. Tommy held a tiny plastic dolphin between two fingers, and he was raising it up in the air and diving it down again, squealing, "Splash! Splash! Ker-splash!"

"Hello, Philippe. We're so excited to see your niece dance." Lauren had her hair down, and she looked so much less severe than she did with the tight bun perched on top of her head. "Who's your friend?"

This, too, introducing my boyfriend to my brand new BFF, was completely uncharted territory for me. "Uh, Lauren, I'd like you to meet Sophie's choreographer, Dario Pereira." She made a big show of gawking down to where our hands were joined. "Oh… and my boyfriend. Dario's my boyfriend too."

Lauren and Dario smiled at each other. Dario extended the hand that wasn't holding mine, and Lauren reached for it to shake, and said, "Philippe is a lovely man."

"Yes, he is." Dario squeezed my fingers and then looked at Tommy. "And who is this?"

"This is Tommy... one part little boy and two parts dolphin." Tommy went wild over my introduction. He flapped his arms and squeaked a couple of times.

"Well, I'm happy to meet you, Tommy." Dario bent over and took a closer look at the boy's toy. "Is that a dolphin you have there?"

"Uh huh. Flip always says I'm more than halfway a dolphin. That's cuz I swim so good." Tommy was nothing short of adorable. "You can see me swim if you come up to the roof pool." Focusing his attention again on the tiny plastic dolphin, he slipped easily back into his game.

"Hey, all! Sorry we're late. The traffic was killer... but you are New Yorkers so you're used to that." Henri burst through the door, and Sophie slipped in quietly behind him. "Introduce me to your girlfriends, Soph."

Sophie dragged him along the line of girls, one-by-one, and Henri bent down and smiled at each one in a way that appeared to be warm, but I could tell he was sizing them up, asking himself, are these girls good enough to be friends with my daughter? And after he'd met them, he came right over to where I stood with Dario, Lauren, and Tommy. The "sizing up" continued as Henri's eyes traced Dario from top to bottom. I wasn't sure if he was asking himself whether Dario was good enough to teach his daughter to dance or to sleep with his little brother. But there were questions in his eyes.

"Henri Bergeron? I am Dario Pereira. We have spoken on the phone quite a lot, and it is nice to finally be able to put a face to the voice."

Henri just nodded politely, not yet ready to pass judgment on Dario, if I knew my brother at all. He'd have to observe Dario for a while before he'd commit to liking him... or disliking him, for that matter. But the two men shook hands. That was when Tommy caught Henri's eye. And I immediately recognized the flash of pain as my brother's eyes flickered over the boy's blond head. Because four years ago, Henri had lost a little blond son of his own, when he was just about Tommy's age.

I stepped forward. "Henri, these are my friends, Lauren and Tommy. Lauren Davis, and Tommy, meet my brother Henri."

Lauren and Henri smiled at each other courteously, but it couldn't be denied that Henri was having trouble keeping his eyes off Tommy.

"Well, how about if we get started with the dancing?" Dario took over, which was a relief to me.

SOPHIE'S PERFORMANCE was so... so purely and completely Sophie. She was a wistful and sweet ballerina, twirling and leaping delicately in the brightest sunshine. But occasionally, and at very opportune moments in the music, she morphed into a snarky, sassy creature of darkness... at least that's the way I saw it. And during those brief spells when she was the dark Sophie, her back bent into a wide arching curve, her toes flexed upward, her fingers resembling claws, she danced with passion and commitment and even anger. In other words, Sophie played the parts of both Beauty *and* the Beast. She spent most of the dance as the sweet young Beauty, but there lingered a hurt and raging Beast just beneath the surface that she portrayed convincingly. I couldn't help but wonder if this was the angry part of Sophie who had lost her mother and brother far too soon.

When the haunting music stopped and Sophie finally stilled, Sophie's friends jumped to their feet and rushed to surround her.

"That's an amazing solo!"

"Will you choreograph one for me, Dario?"

"You'll get into any college you want with that solo, Sophie!"

Tommy and Lauren clapped with enthusiasm, but Henri... well, he was *affected*. Really affected, and I could relate, having been there myself. He stood up and looked from Dario to Sophie and back to Dario again.

"All I can say is," he cleared his throat, rubbed his eyes, and continued, "that was marvelous! I'm astonished that you were able to *see* Sophie so well... and to infuse her personality into that solo."

Dario simply smiled. If he was relieved to be off the hook, it didn't show on his face. "Thank you, Henri. I am very happy that you like it."

Sophie looked at her father. "So you liked it, Dad?"

He moved to her side and gave her one of his fierce bear hugs. "I can't believe my eyes... not that I didn't think you were capable... because I knew you were all along... but...." It wasn't often that Henri was at a loss for words. He loosened his hold on Sophie and announced to the entire room, "I'm taking this whole crowd out for dinner at Nougatine—the restaurant at the Trump International Hotel and Tower. One Central Park West. Be there as soon as you can!" Then he was fumbling through his jacket pockets for his iPhone, and next thing I knew he was on his phone, demanding reservations for nine in that commanding tone of voice I was so used to.

Before Dario and I started folding up the chairs to stack in the corner, I saw my brother lean down and say something into Lauren's ear. She looked up and laughed, and together they watched as Sophie and her friends scooped Tommy up and whisked him from the room.

20

I WOULDN'T say that I'd exactly been freaked out over the fact that Dario and I had said we loved each other, but I would admit that I was having some trouble coming to terms with what it meant in the big picture of my life.

Who am I now that I love a man and he loves me back?

It was hard to call yourself a loner when you had a lover and a best friend, even if they were both found within the same man. And that was what I had in Dario: a person who I really liked and could relate to, as well as one who was so hot that I had actually caught myself drooling while simply thinking about him. And someone I respected deeply.

I *liked* and *loved* and *wanted* Dario Pereira.

And I wasn't sure how those facts fit into the life I'd been leading.

So, as I wrestled with my lone-wolf-in-love quandary, I also stood waiting in the crowded lobby of Steps on Broadway for Sophie and Dario to finish this little dynamo of a French ballerina's floor barre class and scanning the headshots of the school's many dance teachers that were posted on the main wall.

"Those men are quite handsome men, aren't they, bear cub?"

I recognized that haughty voice, and I couldn't prevent my resulting full-body cringe.

"And that's because they know what to do with a razor and a can of shaving cream—I mean, *seriously, dude,* have you looked in a mirror lately?"

I turned around to see the long-legged, smooth-cheeked, Nordic-hunk Kenny Larson, one hand on his hip, evaluating me critically. Of course, I could come up with no clever comeback.

"Don't go thinking that Dario Pereira takes you seriously—not even for a minute. I mean, how could he? The man's an artist—he recognizes beauty and perfection. In fact, I'm gonna let you in on a little secret: that man has more talent in his pinky finger than the rest of us have in our grandest dreams. But you, Grizzly Adams, if your goal is to snag Dario, you're entering into a pissing contest with yours truly. And it's a contest you have absolutely no hope of winning."

Come to think of it, I'd never been able to put together those biting and witty comebacks that were so necessary to survival in middle and high school. But everybody in my hometown knew me as "that pathetic boy whose mother croaked," so the other kids, for the most part, took it easy on me. We weren't, however, in my hometown middle school right now.

"You think he's going to walk into a classy dance convention hall with Big Foot hanging on his arm? Don't make me laugh." But it was too late, because he was already laughing at me.

"I... uh, I-I don't think...."

"That's right, you little troll, you *didn't* think about what havoc your hairy ass could wreak on his career. So why don't you grab that lame backpack of yours and leave Dario to the people who can actually be there for him in the ways he needs."

Kenny was beautiful and blond and looked almost angelic, but he proved time and time again that he was no angel. And although my most primal instinct told me to book it down the three flights of stairs and onto the city street where I could blend into the crowd as I had done once before under a strikingly similar circumstance, instead, I stopped to think the situation through. I remembered something Dario had told me: he'd said that he worked in a very superficial world. I decided that maybe this was the kind of thing he was talking about.

"I have enough respect for Dario to let him make his own decisions about who he hangs out with." I actually had to stop, take a deep breath, and remind myself that my balls hadn't appeared to be any smaller than any of the other guys' balls that I'd seen in my high school locker room when we were stripping down to take a shower after gym class, way back when. And after doing that, I found the strength inside me to stare back at Kenny Larson.

At that moment class was let out, and I looked back into the studio, watching as Sophie and Dario gravitated toward each other and then moved to the front of the room like they belonged together. Dario said a few words to the tiny ballet mistress and then introduced Sophie, who bobbed into a quick curtsy. I could feel Kenny's glare drilling into my back right between my shoulder blades, watching me as I watched them. And as soon as Dario was out of the classroom, Kenny was right in his face, his back turned rudely to Sophie.

"Dari, you looked fabulous in there... and don't you dare think for a minute that I missed the sight of those gorgeous abs hidden underneath that T-shirt. You can't hide that six pack from me, mister!" He poked at Dario's belly. I turned away so I didn't have to see any more because it hurt like hell to see Kenny touch, so casually, the man I'd admitted that I loved. Unfortunately, though, I could still *hear* him clearly. "I have a few things I'd like to discuss with you about Herman's piece. So how about I treat you to a little lunch at Gigi's Cafe?"

"Cannot do it, Kenny. In fact, I already have *two* dates for lunch." Dario reached behind Kenny and pulled Sophie around so she was beside him once again. "And I am sure you did not *intentionally* present your back to Sophie."

Guilty, Kenny giggled. "Of course not." He gave Soph a distracted hug. "How are you, dear? You don't mind if Dari takes a rain check on your lunch date today, do you? We have business to review."

I heard the very start of Sophie's stuttered reply before Dario put a quick end to Kenny's game. "I *said* I have plans, Kenny. We can talk about anything that needs to be reviewed before class tomorrow. Come on, Sophie. Let's say hello to Philippe—he's waiting for us."

And as simple as that, Dario had shut down Kenny's advances. When he reached my side, I got a quick peck on my furry cheek and a suggestive comment in my ear that made me blush.

"Hi, Phil. That guy, Kenny—he's an asshole."

"Soph! You better watch your language or your dad is going to blame your newly acquired trash mouth on too much time spent with me!" I had to smile, though; first, because I knew for a fact that she hadn't acquired so much as a single curse from the language I used, and second, because it appeared that Sophie was coming out of her shell... and then some.

"When, in fact, she learned all of her trash talk from *me*!" Dario was enjoying seeing me sweat, maybe just a little bit too much.

"Guys, I'm gonna go wash up a bit and get dressed. I'll be out in a few minutes, and I'm frigging starving so be ready to head out to lunch." Sophie and her truck driver mouth took off to the ladies' changing room.

Dario watched her trot away, and then he leaned in close to me. "I saw that you had company while you were waiting for us."

I looked down at the floor, wanting to avoid the topic of Kenny, but Dario took my chin in hand and raised my face back up so I couldn't hide from him.

"What did he say to you?"

I lowered my head again as soon as he dropped his hand from my face, kicked at one booted foot with the other, and frowned. "Same you-know-what, different day... it's not a problem."

"Anything that puts *this* look on your face is a problem for me." He turned to Kenny, who looked pissed-off enough to spit nails about the fact that Dario wasn't going to lunch with him. "Kenny, listen to me very carefully. I am rather a jealous sort of man. If you do not mind, I would appreciate it if you would stay away far from my lover while I am in class. I cannot concentrate when I see him out in the hall with another man." Dario said it so seriously that *I* almost believed it. "Come to the changing room with me, Philippe. I want to keep an eye on you." He took my hand with a quick wink, and we headed to the men's locker room.

"Did you catch a load of his face? He's not happy with you at all."

Dario stopped and then turned me around kind of roughly so that I was facing him. "Go ahead, Phil, ask me if I care."

I shook my head and tried to keep walking.

"Ask me." He'd planted his feet in the middle of the hallway and was hanging onto my arm with one tight fist—I had a gut feeling we wouldn't be going anywhere until I did what he'd suggested.

"Okay... okay...." Dario was about the most stubborn man I'd ever met, except, maybe, for Henri. "Dario, do you care that your friend Kenny is mad as a hatter at you?"

He reached up, touched the side of my face, and said, "I am so glad you asked." I cracked up laughing at the innocent way he said it. "I do not care in the slightest that Kenny is seeing red, because the man I love is smiling again. *Anything* is worth seeing you smile, Philippe."

For a second or two, all I could do was gawk at him. He'd fallen for me so quickly and completely—it was as if he needed our connection as much as I did.

"Not only that, but I would not miss a meal with my two favorite people if Kenny had offered to pay me. You and Sophie and me—we are kind of like our own little family—don't you think?" This time it was Dario's turn to blush and look away from me, like he couldn't believe he'd let those words slip.

But he'd said them, and at hearing those words, I got this warm feeling—it flooded all over me like I'd just stepped into a sauna. For some reason, I kind of shivered before I stepped forward to hug him. "I... I l-love you too." And at that moment, everything inside of my heart and my head changed. It was like God had flicked a switch and I was suddenly okay with how I felt about Dario... *and* with saying goodbye to my loner status.

I was more than okay with it, really, because it felt right.

21

"OKAY, PHILIPPE. I need your full attention."

I pulled off my T-shirt and dropped it on the lounge chair next to Lauren's. Tommy was already playing by the side of the pool. "What's up?"

"Sit down, sweetie. I have a proposition for you."

"That sounds dangerous." Nonetheless, I plopped down onto the chair beside her and then pulled my hair into a low ponytail because I knew that my hair got me hot really fast if I sat in the sun for any length of time. "So what's up?"

For a minute, we just watched quietly as Tommy filled up a plastic cup with pool water, emptied it over his toes, and then did it again. Finally, she said, "Well, first of all, I found a job."

I shifted my eyes off Tommy to look at Lauren. "That's great! Where?"

"At an investments firm in the financial district. I'll fill you in on all of the details later, but just know that this is a good job... a very big job. And that leaves me with a big problem."

"Why? You're all set now, Lauren—you found an apartment and a job—what more could you want?"

"I want excellent childcare for Tommy."

"Well, yeah, of course." She was looking at me strangely. "That goes without saying."

"I want you."

I sat up straighter. "Huh?"

"I want you to stay in New York City... and be Tommy's nanny... or manny... or whatever you want to call it." She appeared uncertain. "I think it would work out well for all three of us."

I had one of those get-up-and-run urges that I fought on a regular basis, but somehow, I found it easier than usual to push back. I was getting better and better at doing that lately. "What do you mean?"

That was when she spun around and sat up on the edge of her chair. "What I mean is, I need a nanny—you need a job. I want Tommy to be cared for by someone who loves him—you love Tommy. You'd need a place to stay—I, conveniently, have a spare room in my new apartment. That's what I mean."

"So let me get this straight: you want me to be your live-in child-care provider?"

"God, Phil, you make it sound like a crime, or something."

I slid my backside off my own chair and dropped it onto Lauren's chair beside her. "I'm an unemployed fisherman with no education or experience with children whatsoever and—"

"And you love Tommy. *That* is what he needs—someone who loves him, and who he loves in return. Not someone 'professional.'" She made an air quote gesture.

I looked over at her; she was studying me with every bit of the intensity that Dario always did. "You're serious, aren't you?"

"As serious as... as serious as a mother can be about doing what is best for her child." Her eyes grew wide and hopeful, which struck a chord in my heart.

"I don't know what to say."

"Well, I can help you with that, buddy. Say, 'sounds like a fantastic idea, Lauren, you genius.'"

I stood up and looked over at Tommy. It would be awesome to watch him every day as he grew up. To take him to the playground, to the zoo, and even to dance shows where his mind could be opened up to music and movement, the way mine had been opened this summer.

He looked up at me and waved. "Hiya, Flip!"

I waved back to him.

Other implications of what Lauren was offering me rushed into my mind. Sure, I'd been offered a job and a home, but I'd also been offered a way to hold onto my relationship with Dario.

"And remember that one time, how you told me you were interested in looking into possibly being a teacher someday? Early childhood education, right?"

I nodded; I *had* told her that. Spending time helping out with Sophie and Tommy this summer had felt right to me. Like it fit with who I was. And at one point it had crossed my mind that maybe I was meant to help people, or, more specifically, to work with kids. I'd actually confessed my big idea to Lauren one morning by the pool. It looked like now it was coming back to haunt me.

"Well, you could take education classes in the evenings, or maybe part-time during the day, depending on how I set up my own work schedule."

She has it all planned out, doesn't she?

"So? Don't clam up on me, dammit. Be the new man in my life… in the babysitter/BFF way, of course."

From where I was standing, I had an excellent view of the city skyline, the place that I could call my new home if I chose to. "I'll think it over, Lauren. But I'll need a bit of time."

Lauren hugged me. "I'm sure you'll make the right decision and be moving your crap into our new apartment as of September first."

22

IT TOOK us only a half hour or so on the Red Line to get to the Nevins Street stop in Brooklyn. Dario had taken a day off of his New Jersey studio's summer dance classes to come along with us to the Mark Morris Dance Center. Over the past several years, he'd attended many classes here and had even taken part in the Mark Morris Pre-Professional Summer Intensive during the summer after his junior year in high school, so he knew the building well enough to show us around. Earlier that week, he had made a call confirming that it would be okay if he took us inside.

The first thought that entered my mind when I saw the Mark Morris Dance Center building was "holy crap!", but I'd seen enough examples of eclectic artistic expressions since I'd been in the city exploring the world of dance with Sophie to be able to put it into perspective. One outside wall of the building was covered entirely with a brightly colored mural, showing what looked to be names and initials scattered among three-D designs. I would have expected the mural on a community dance center to depict giant dancers, but instead, it seemed like an individual artist's statement.

"Someone told me that the artist's name is Barry McGee—he's a painter and graffiti artist—and he created a sort of autobiography in this mural. I do not think it is meant to say anything specific about the neighborhood or politics or even about dance... which I find rather intriguing."

"What is 'Fong'? Why is it painted so big—see, right over there, and up there, too?" Sophie pointed, as taken with the mural as Dario was. Okay, and me. I really liked the mural too.

"I'm fairly certain that it is one of the monikers, or nicknames, Barry McGee uses as a painter."

"The whole thing is awesome—it makes me want to go inside." Sophie snapped a few pictures of the mural with the camera on her phone.

"Then let's go in."

The inside of the building was just as impressive. As we headed through the lobby, Dario explained that it had been a derelict building in the neighborhood when the Mark Morris Dance Group bought it; the renovations had taken almost two years to complete. Once in the building, there was a clean, modern feeling: a lot of blue and white, the ceilings were all very high, with plenty of windows, contributing to a bright, almost weightless feeling inside. Many of the hallway walls were decorated with movement photography, blurred images of dancers taken by Mikhail Baryshnikov, himself.

In all, there were seven studios in the building, but Dario took us to one that he called "Duffy," which was both a studio and performance space. It was enormous, with high ceilings, a black Marley floor, and a piano in the corner. As our visit had been expected, some chairs were set up in a corner, so we sat down quietly and watched the company rehearse. The first thing I noticed was that music was at the center of their work.

Dario seemed to have read my mind. "This company is very musical. Mark Morris, himself, is a conductor, so these dancers have to know how to count."

At this point, they were rehearsing a piano piece. Not being an expert on dance, my overall impression was that the piece was eclectic, at times, even funny, and entertaining to me, an average Joe. The movements were all complex, and there was a lot of fluid motion, like a sort of prancing and even some rolling on the floor. There were also some movements that didn't look to be dance steps, but instead, simply motions that showed the choreographer's vision.

Once seated, the three of us didn't say much to one another, and although Mark Morris wasn't there at the rehearsal, it was clearly a very strict environment. We slipped out after about an hour, and even when we were back out on the street, both Sophie and Dario's eyes were still as large as dinner plates.

As we headed back to the subway, they chatted. "I really loved what I saw in there, Dario."

"I know. It's unbelievable, isn't it? Mark Morris is truly a genius. I would love to work for his company, but most of their dancers have educations from SUNY Purchase and Juilliard."

"So it'd probably be best for me to keep the Mark Morris training in the back of my mind, for after college."

"True, but they offer short intensives. Maybe next summer, you and I could do the summer intensive here in Brooklyn together."

Next summer? He thinks that the three of us are still going to know each other next summer?

"Yeah… that'd be awesome!" Sophie immediately pulled out her phone and began to text her friends.

He turned to me. "How did you like the dancing, Philippe?"

"It blew my mind. Those dancers are so talented… and athletic."

Dario looked a little bit worried. "I hope someday you will be coming to see me dance in a company like that."

He's talking about the future again, like he assumes that this isn't going be over between us when the summer comes to an end.

"Uh… yeah. I probably will."

I would swear he winced visibly, as if I'd hurt his feelings with my noncommittal response. But he quickly recovered. "Of course you will. I will save you a front row seat at every show." Dario grabbed my hand and squeezed it, which surprised me. I turned to look at him.

The vulnerability I saw in his eyes made my breath catch in my throat. His expression was so open, so intense, so exposed—and he wasn't trying to hide it from me at all. "You and Sophie are like a family to me and… and I-I never really had one of my own before."

It was suddenly as plain as day to me: Dario Pereira, an orphaned Brazilian-American boy who had been carefully placed in a foster home in a Brazilian community in Somerville, Massachusetts, so he could feel as if he belonged but had never fully bonded there, had found a family with Sophie and me.

THROUGHOUT THE rest of the day, every now and then, I thought about the remark Dario had made earlier about family. And I was glad he'd made it, because I'd learned something valuable from it. He'd confided in me today that, with Soph and me, for the first time ever, he felt like he had a family. And at lunch one day the week before, Dario had told me that he defined *family* as people who cared about you, not because it was their court-appointed duty to do so, but just because they wanted to. His simple way of viewing the subject of family really made me think. A family wasn't necessarily a group of people related to you by blood, fulfilling traditional roles of "mother, father, and child," but instead, it was the feeling of being *one* that people who spent a lot of time together and depended on each other shared. According to Dario's thought pattern, my quirky family unit—Henri, Sophie and me—with our glaring shortage of mothers, more than qualified.

In the coolness of the hotel room, Dario and I lounged together on the bed, doing, more or less, our own thing. He was scribbling messy notes on a piece of scrap paper, trying to figure out what type of combination he was going to teach in a contemporary class he was subbing for at Steps on Broadway this week. While he was doing that, I was researching City College of New York, checking into the teacher education programs. So far I'd found out that CCNY was the oldest public school of education in New York City, and as for its education program, CCNY had a nationwide reputation for innovation. I had plans to check out the admission requirements for myself, as well as for Sophie, because if she planned to study dance at Mark Morris Dance Group or Martha Graham Dance Foundation, Henri would expect her to also enroll in a school where she could get a bachelor's degree.

But the way Dario was looking at me when I glanced over at him caught my attention and had me sticking my laptop on the bedside table. What I saw in his eyes promised a great deal more in the way of stimulation than I could get from www.ccny.cuny.edu.

"I want to try something new tonight."

A chill ran up my spine. "You do?"

"It involves putting the privacy sign on the door."

I wasn't sure if the first chill up my spine was from anticipation or mild anxiety, but it was soon followed by a second chill.

"And I think I am going to do just that." Dario got up and went to the door. On his way back to the bed, he pulled his T-shirt over his head and dropped it onto the floor. "I want you naked." Without any hesitation at all, he came over to me and started to unbutton my shorts. Before I knew it, he was tugging on them, along with my boxers underneath, until they both slid down my legs. "I want to watch you unbutton your shirt. Look at me while you are doing it."

I wasn't being offered a choice, and frankly, I liked it that way. I followed his directions as best I could with him returning my stare so hungrily, but my eyes soon flickered toward the floor.

"I told you to look at me." I lifted my eyes back up to his face and noted that he wasn't smiling. He sat beside me on the bed, watching my eyes intently. "Now throw your shirt on the floor."

Again, I obeyed without a word. It seemed as if by magic Dario produced condoms and lubricant.

"Philippe, I'm not going to be a selfish lover with you. And I want you to experience what it is like to top another man."

I coughed a couple of times, nervous as hell. "You w-what?"

"You heard me." And with those words, Dario began to prepare his own body for what would come next. And as he did that, which I will admit was quite erotic to witness, he continued to speak. "Now, I consider myself to be a natural top. It's how I am most comfortable when making love, but I am all for give and take in a relationship."

"I... I-uh...."

"That is not to say I won't top as the bottom." He smiled as he admitted, "which is what I am probably going to end up doing tonight. Now, lie down flat on your back, Philippe."

As soon as I was in the right position, he pushed my legs wide apart, knelt sort of boldly between my knees, and looked at me plainly. I wasn't even slightly hard, which was more than a little bit embarrassing. "I-I don't know why... I'm not... you know..."

"Performance anxiety?" He grinned, then licked his lips and bent over me. "I can fix that." For a second, I could feel his warm breath on my dick. Then he lowered his head and took me in; within thirty seconds, I was moaning.

"That didn't take too much effort, did it?" He pulled his lips from my groin, quickly unrolled a condom onto my erection, and then began to climb up my body. As he did, I felt my erection wilt. So Dario pulled the condom off, and repeated the previous step, but when he attempted to position himself so I could enter him from underneath, the same thing happened to me again.

I was mortified. I pulled my hands up to cover my face, not getting what was going on and why my body wasn't cooperating.

This was Dario! The guy I liked and loved and wanted.

What is going on here?

Dario rolled off me to my side. He then pulled my hands from where they were stuck to my face and said softly, his lips against my temple, "Tell me exactly what you are thinking right now."

Once more, he kissed my forehead quickly and then pulled back so he could watch my face when I answered. Dario, as usual, would settle for nothing less than all of me. I met his gaze, but doing it took all of my willpower, because I was so embarrassed. "I'm thinking that I just don't get why this is happening to me."

"Okay. And what else? Tell me what else is on your mind."

"That I'm really turned on by you... but...."

"But what, Philippe?"

I exhaled very slowly to buy time and then admitted in a quiet voice, "I was thinking that I liked making love the way we did it before." I couldn't look at him after I'd disclosed that fact.

For a second, Dario appeared to be thinking, and then he asked, "You like it when I top you?"

Some part of me suspected that I should be humiliated by admitting this, but still I shrugged and then nodded. Because it was the truth, and that was what Dario had asked me to always give him. "But I'll do whatever you want to do... and I'm sure that if we give it another try, I'll be able to—"

"Philippe," Dario interrupted my rambling. "I enjoy making love *most* when I top. I just wanted you to know that we could switch—we still can—whenever you want to." I looked up at him and saw that his expression had become fierce. "But I won't lie to *you* either—when I'm inside you, I'm just where I want to be. *I* want to set our pace. I like to have control."

I could hardly believe what I'd done: I'd just let Dario see the vulnerable person underneath the bushy hair and unruly beard. I'd informed him that I liked to be submissive in bed, which was something I'd just figured out myself, seeing as I was a virgin until a few weeks ago.

And now I was going to ask him for what I wanted. "Then will you? Will you go ahead and do that? Please Dario, take charge like... I want you to just take me...." I needed him so much. And that seemed to be more than fine with him, because my lover allowed a smile. Not a big and bright grin, but much more of a small, seductive smirk.

"Try to stop me." Dario lifted his athletic body so he was on his knees, and simply by the greedy way he was regarding me as he knelt there, I knew he was going to deliver exactly what I'd just requested. His muscular thighs flexing with effort, Dario moved forward and then lifted one over me and straddled my chest, little by little allowing his weight to press my shoulders into the mattress. That was when told me exactly how it was going to be. "You will take what I give to you." I barely had a chance to nod when he shifted his body so his chiseled bronze hips were pushed directly in front of my face, his dick pointing at my lips. The next thing I knew, he had taken himself in hand, and was feeding his dick to me.

As I struggled to take all of him inside my mouth and throat, shivers of pleasure and rightness and thrill made their way up my spine... and up my arms and legs, as well. The way he took exactly what he needed from my mouth, how he moved at his own pace, speeding up to a frenzied tempo and then slowing down to near stillness as it suited him, proved to bring me to a level of arousal that had my butt squirming and my legs squeezing together in a need I'd never before known.

I wanted more, but I knew it wasn't my role to ask. I would take what I was given, as Dario had instructed. But he must have sensed my need. Brushing the side of my face tenderly with one flattened palm, he slowly removed his flesh from my mouth and slid back over to lie by my side, dragging his strong leg back over my chest. I watched his eyes, certainly with eagerness, but still wary of what would come next.

Then Dario reached behind me, his fingers somehow already moistened with lube, and got me ready to take him. "Turn over onto your stomach, Philippe. It'll be so good that way." His voice was calm and gentle... but firm.

As soon as I flipped over and he had taken care of protecting us with a condom, he covered me with his body. And as he pushed inside me, I could feel the even puffs of his warm breath heaving softly on the back of my neck.

I admitted with a small sob, "I don't know just why it is...."

"Why you like me on top of you... and inside you?"

Thankfully, he couldn't see the way my cheeks reddened at his question. "Yeah... I don't... oh, God... I don't know why...." It just felt so good, and I hadn't yet mastered the art of taking my pleasure in stride, so I couldn't string even a simple sentence together while he was thrusting into me so steadily.

"Maybe...." Dario was starting to breath more heavily now, but I could still hear the smile in his voice. "Maybe it is because... I see who you are... and you know you are safe here... with me... and you are where... you belong." Dario reached under me and gripped my dick like it belonged to him. "Yes—you're exactly where you belong—*that's why.*"

That was pretty much the extent of our conversation. I then just closed my eyes tight and let myself tumble into this feeling I'd just realized I craved: the freedom that came with giving up my control to somebody I trusted.

"I love you so much, Philippe... don't forget that you belong to me."

He was right, and I was now officially out of hiding.

23

HENRI HAD arranged for a gift to thank Dario for the wonderful solo he had choreographed for Sophie. He had sent us to *Annie The Musical* at the Palace Theatre in Times Square. It had thrilled all three of us. The sound of those little girls' voices blasting throughout the theater was at first shocking, and then exhilarating. Dario and I sat with our hands squeezed tightly together from the beginning of the performance until its very end. And Sophie was so adorable—her expression throughout the entire musical reminded me of when she was a little kid.

After the musical, we went to the Roxy Delicatessen for a late dinner; it was pretty much the only place in Times Square that could seat us at that point. We followed the host to our table upstairs, and after Sophie finished her texting frenzy—she'd had her phone turned off for the entire length of the musical, so she had some catching up with her friends to do—we ordered a bunch of different appetizers to share.

"Please thank your father again for me. He really did not have to send us to a musical... but I am so glad he did...."

Sophie laughed, and then she sort of whined, "Me, too. You guys, I don't want to go back to Massachusetts." She looked back and forth from Dario to me. "I love it here... and Dario, I'm gonna miss you so much! You've kind of turned into another uncle to me this summer."

Dario blushed—the shade of pink was so bright it showed up easily despite his brown skin. "W-well, thank you, Sophie. You don't know what that means to me."

"Can we come back and visit every few weekends, huh, Phil?"

Both of them looked at me with genuine interest. I rarely spoke of my plans, seeing as until recently, I didn't have any. "Well, maybe you can come stay with me... here... in the city."

Both of their chins dropped at once. "What are you talking about?" Again, Sophie was the one to speak.

"I, uh…I planned to bring this up with you guys tonight. So… here it is: Lauren offered me a job as Tommy's child-care provider. And she has an extra bedroom in her apartment. She invited me to move in with them."

I heard two individual gasps from my little audience.

"I haven't said yes yet. I asked for some time to think it over."

"Say yes, Phil! *So* say yes! You love it here, and Dario is here, and I can visit you and…."

By now, Dario's pink face had dulled down to a kind of stunned-looking, pale brown. He appeared to be beyond words. *I* was very familiar with the feeling, but it wasn't Dario's usual manner.

I needed to know how he felt about me staying and about me being a more… a more permanent part of his life. "How do *you* feel about me sticking around, Dario?"

His response wasn't at all what I expected. That is to say, it wasn't calm, cool, and collected, like the normal Dario. He jumped up, sort of flew across the table, and was sitting in my lap inside the space of a second. "Stay, Philippe… I want you to stay." His eyes told me even more than his actions (which, all alone, spoke quite clearly); I saw inside them this strange combination of demanding and pleading that was completely new.

I ran my hand through his silky black hair, and then down the back of his dark gray dress shirt, stopping only when I reached his belt. "I'm still thinking about it, like I said. But… but I plan on giving Lauren an answer in the next few days."

Sophie was already making plans for *when*, not *if*, I lived here. "When I do my college auditions, I can stay with you too. That'll be way better than a hotel. And Lauren is so nice, and I *love* little Tommy." Before I knew it, she was texting again.

"Sophie…." I tried to send her a reminder that I hadn't decided yet, but she was well beyond that, her attention now fully focused on her phone. So I spoke into Dario's ear. "You really want to have me around all the time?"

He didn't turn on my lap to look back at me. Apparently recovered from his excitement, he answered in true Dario fashion, "I already said that I did, Philippe."

"If I stay, I might take some education classes at City College."

"You have a gentle, caring nature, Phil. You *will* make an excellent teacher."

I will?

"Everything has changed for me in the past six weeks, know what I mean?" I had to make him understand that this was all so new to me.

"I think I do."

"It's like life doesn't hurt as much as it did before."

I waited for his response, but he remained quiet, as if he was hoping I'd say more.

So I did. "Before I got here, to the city, all I wanted to do was get lost... or at least, to stay in the shadows."

"I've told you before—you cannot hide from me, Philippe." That claim was spoken with a fierceness I now recognized.

"I know... and I don't really want to. It's like, I've decided to take this risk—to let myself love you and *need* you, even—and, sure, I'm kind of terrified, but it's worth it to me." The only problem was that, sure, I'd come clean about my feelings, but I was still hiding "the big thing," and I knew it. I hadn't mentioned the devastating and lasting effect my mother's death had on me—and the resulting depression I couldn't seem to fully shake. *Even now.*

"Anything you do, besides sitting alone in your hotel room, involves taking a risk. I am just glad you are taking the risk on me."

I was still hugging him against my chest when our food got there.

Before he got up to go back to his seat, he kissed my cheek and said softly, "This is what it means to love somebody." I couldn't tell if he was asking me or telling me. But the way he said those words reminded me that Dario was taking a risk with his heart, as well.

24

WE WERE only going to be there for one more week. It had been an eye-opening summer on many levels, for both Sophie and me. Sophie had become familiar with the New York City dance scene. While continuing to polish up her ballet skills, she had sampled different modern dance techniques and tried her hand at contemporary dance. She had made friends and kept them. She had uncovered the secrets of some of the city's most famous dance programs and gotten a feel for several college dance curricula. Overall, I'd say that Sophie had met Henri's main objective and separated herself quite a ways from her protective shell.

And me... well, even if I hadn't spilled out the true source of my lingering inner pain to Dario, I had put some distance between myself and my shell too. And tonight, I was going to meet Lauren and Tommy and Dario for dinner at the hotel, with Sophie in tow, of course, and I was going to accept the job and the living arrangements that Lauren had offered. And right at the table, I supposed, we would place a call on speakerphone to Henri to let him know that my days on the fishing boat were in the past.

Win-win-win-win-win situation, all around.

That morning, the three of us had been at DANY Studios on 38th and 8th so Dario could put some finishing touches on Sophie's solo. Since it was a nice day outside, sunny and on the cool side, we'd decided to walk back through Hell's Kitchen to the Holiday Inn and then go for a quick swim before Dario and Sophie had to get back to their dance classes.

IT HAPPENED really quickly. It was 11:47 a.m., at the intersection of 46th Street and 9th Avenue. Between the Yum Yum Too Restaurant and the Yum Yum Three... Thai food, for the record.

It's funny how little details like these stick in your mind.

That was my exact location when my world crashed for the second time.

BETWEEN THESE two Yum Yum restaurants, there was a cement island/divider kind of thing, floating in the middle of the street. All three of us somehow ended up perched rather precariously on it, waiting for the light to change. Dario was standing right next to me—that is, until he wasn't.

Which was because he was suddenly lying on the fucking street with some dude on a bike bending over him, wailing something like, "I'm so sorry! I didn't mean to drag him into the street... I think his arm got caught in my backpack!"

This next part happened in slow motion.

A bunch of cars had kind of pooled up around where Dario lay, there was a lot of honking—some cars were trying desperately to squeeze past, as if a body in the street was no reason to take pause. Sophie had practically flung herself on top of Dario and was shaking his shoulders, screaming over and over, "Are you all right? Are you all right?" A crowd of pedestrians had formed a semicircle around him. A few people lifted their phones, maybe to dial 9-1-1, but one guy in an I LOVE NY T-shirt used his phone to snap a picture of Dario, as if he had been placed flat out on his back on 46th Street, bleeding from the back of the head, as some kind of a tourist attraction.

In that one stretched-out moment of mind-numbing panic, I had a moment of complete clarity. And with it came the knowledge that I had made a huge mistake. I was completely and totally out of my league in what I had been attempting to do with Dario. I turned to the side and vomited on the street, causing some of the fast-intruding spectators to back off a bit. Then I froze... and I began to separate myself from the emotions that were fast encroaching upon me... threatening to take me down.

"Oh my God, Dario! Oh, my God!" I recognized Sophie's voice. But it was as if I was hearing it from underwater. "Uncle Phil—help me! Help us!"

From my newly acquired seat up on the moon, I surveyed the entire situation. I saw the crowd, the cars, the bicyclist, Sophie kneeling on the pavement, a very still body.

Too still. Way too fucking still for me to make myself return to Earth from the distant location at which I'd parked my consciousness.

And then that still body moved. It started with the fingers: just a tiny twitch or two... really hard to say from way up there in space.

Maybe Dario's not dead. It took a moment for that realization to sink into my dazed brain.

"Dario, are you all right? God, you got dragged into the street and...." That was Sophie, but I still heard her as if from deep under water.

His eyes popped open, shocking me slightly, which was hard to do, considering that I was already in a complete state of shock, and then I watched as he struggled to lift his beautiful dancer's body from its deathly pose. First his elbows bent, and he shakily held the weight of his upper body on them for a moment, and then a couple of bystanders moved to either side of him and pulled him up to his feet. Once standing, Dario wobbled quite a bit, but thankfully, his rescuers didn't let him go.

They were everything I couldn't be right then. Strong, calm, self-assured.

I took a step back and hid behind my hair.

"Hey, mister, do you need an ambulance?" one of the rescuers asked Dario.

He shook his head slowly.

Dead people can't do that. Dead people never answer your questions.

"Well, there's gonna be an ambulance here soon, I'm pretty sure I can hear it coming. If you stick around, you're gonna be heading to the hospital, like it or not."

Dario shook his head again, completely disoriented.

"I think you should go to the hospital, Dario. You hit your head... it's bleeding." Sophie had removed her sweater and was pushing it to his scalp.

"I'm okay," he said.

I'm not, I thought.

"I think maybe I passed out for a second, but I am fine now. Where's Philippe?"

I could hear their conversation more clearly now, so I supposed I'd returned from outer space or from under water, or wherever the fuck it was I'd been.

"Uncle Phil, come here!"

And as if I was being drawn in, like a fish on a line, I felt my body move toward them. "I'm coming."

Dario looked up at me, traumatized.

I looked back at him. But when our eyes met, I had no feelings whatsoever.

No feelings of fear.

No feelings of distress.

No anger.

No sick-to-my-stomach, oh-my-God-I-almost-lost-you, I-need-to-purge-myself-of-every-single-bit-of-the-icy-cold-burning-hot-acid-in-my-belly that had somehow managed to paralyze me.

I felt nothing about this fucked-up situation we were in.

I felt nothing for Dario. I couldn't… because if I let myself, I'd lose it.

No, no… like I said, I felt nothing.

Vaguely, I heard my boyfriend utter, "My head hurts. Can I lie down for a while in your hotel room?"

Is he talking to me?

"Of course, Dario. Can you walk okay? Snap out of it, *Uncle Phil*! Get over here and support his weight."

I obeyed Sophie's command.

"Did you get hit by a car?"

"No, Sophie… I think I just got caught on that biker's bag… and got pulled out onto the street. But I hit my head pretty hard on the pavement."

Hearing that, I once again slipped away to where I was safe: a million miles from there.

"Philippe? You're acting strange." That was Dario speaking into a vacuum. Thinking of my needs, when he should be worrying about himself.

I forced myself to reply. "Dario, let's get you back to the hotel." My voice sounded high-pitched and shrill, even to my own ears. When I placed my arm beneath his to support his weight, there was none of the usual electricity I felt when our skin connected. He was simply dead weight. I struggled to help him along.

A few more times on the way home, Sophie and Dario asked *me* about how *I* was doing. *How I was doing....*

I was just fucking dandy.

WE HUNG around the hotel for the rest of the afternoon. None of us were up for swimming. Or talking. We rented a couple of movies and lay on the beds to silently watch them. Sophie called and cancelled our dinner with Lauren and Tommy.

And I planned my escape.

THAT NIGHT, Dario got tired earlier than usual. I guess Sophie just assumed he was going to stay over, because at about nine, she said "Goodnight, boys. And... um, I'm so glad you're okay, Dario."

I stared at her as she walked out, and then I turned my head just enough to stare beside me at the bed where my lover lay.

"You have barely said a word all day, Philippe." His voice shook like he was weary. At the very end, my mother's voice had shaken in much the same way. And she had said essentially the same words to me that Dario just had.

Philippe, honey... you've hardly made a sound all day.

"Do you want a soda before bed?" I asked gruffly.

I am the king of avoidance.

"No. But I do want to know what you are thinking right now—so tell me." I could tell he was trying to be pushy with me, but he was too weak to make his voice sound as insistent as usual.

My first instinct was to start talking as I was a naturally compliant person, not to mention that Dario had established a level of dominance over me, which I had eagerly allowed. I was on the verge of informing him about just how close I'd come as a preteen to taking my own life in the wake of my mother's death… to filling him in on the three-year depression that had left me alive, though nothing but a withdrawn, aching bag of bones at the age of thirteen. And to let him know that seeing him sprawled out lifelessly on the street had changed everything in my heart. And now I had no choice but to shy away from him, as I would from anything or anyone that threatened to bring me back to the destroyed state in which I'd existed as a young teenager. It was a matter of self-preservation—run and hide, or die.

So I shook my head, unwilling to play his game. "There's nothing at all on my mind… except whether or not you'd like a soda."

Dario exhaled loudly, frustrated. "No, I do not want soda. Just come to bed."

Again, a voice inside me screamed, "Run! Hide!" But I was going to hold him one more time, for the last time, tonight.

I crawled into the bed and took Dario in my arms immediately, certain that the memories of this one last night together would end up hurting me more than I'd be able to bear. But I couldn't resist him, and I gave in to the distant part of myself that knew I was still in love with him. I pulled him to me, probably a bit too roughly considering what he'd been through today, and I set about the task of learning every inch of his body that I could touch without arousing him.

That night was not about sex; it was about committing Dario's body to my memory. I sank my nose deep into his hair and took in his scent, because it was yet another thing that I didn't ever intend to forget. And I kissed the back of his neck with an open mouth, tasting his skin, savoring it for the last time.

Then I listened to his breathing as he slept. Even, untroubled… the easy respiration of life, itself. I would leave him now, knowing that he was okay, and because of that, I was *technically* okay too.

At least, I would be okay until the daylight came, and I had to go.

So I didn't sleep at all. I refused to squander my last moments with Dario, unaware of his presence. Very early in the morning, I climbed from the bed, accidentally disturbing him.

"Philippe… why are you getting up so early?" His voice rumbled with sleepiness.

"I'm just going to the bathroom, that's all," I lied.

He nodded, then rolled onto his side and went back to sleep.

Silently, I walked around the room and gathered my belongings, stuffing them haphazardly into my duffel bag. Then I placed the room's key card on the table by the TV. When everything was ready, I found the hotel's notepaper and pen, and I scribbled out a note to Dario.

> *I can't do this. I thought I could, but I just can't. I'm sorry.*
>
> *Please tell Lauren that I can't take the job.*
>
> *And please look after Sophie for the rest of the week. Call Henri, and he will come here to get her on the weekend and take her home.*
>
> *I'm sorry.*

I didn't write how much I loved him, because it really didn't matter at this point. I didn't explain how afraid I was that I'd slip back into the same kind of depression I'd experienced when I'd lost my mother at thirteen. Or the fact that I felt the exact same sense of impending despair crushing in upon me from all sides.

I didn't even sign the note. He'd know exactly which sorry loser it was from.

I consoled myself with the thought that they'd all be better off without me in the end. I left the room without a backward glance.

25

I WISHED that I could have avoided using the credit card Henri had given me for chaperoning Sophie this summer, but because I'd left the debit card to my personal account in the night table drawer at the Holiday Inn, I needed to use it if I wanted to survive. Not that I was 100 percent certain I wanted to survive at this point, but since I hadn't made an official decision to check out (and I wasn't referring to a hotel), I used the card, took enough cash out for a bus trip back to Boston, and headed for the Megabus stop on 34th Street.

I needed to put as much distance as possible between the crushing emotions that came from seeing Dario "dead" on the street, and me. There was really only one place that I could think of to go: back to the ocean.

Within a couple of hours into my bus ride, I had received five voice mails. The first and the last were from Dario. He was shocked at my note and by my actions. I'd devastated him. He'd loved me. And he'd truly thought that I was his family. I had "broken his heart."

The second was from Sophie. She wanted to know what the hell I was thinking. And what was my frigging problem? She didn't understand how I could leave her like that. And she reminded me that Dario was the sweetest and kindest guy on the planet, how could I hurt him? "*Uncle Phil*, you are acting like a world class asshole" was how she summed it up.

Then came Lauren's call. She was puzzled, as well as "entirely pissed off." I'd led her to believe that I'd be taking the job caring for Tommy. She'd told him, and now he was going to be so disappointed. I was just one more guy who had hurt them by leaving them like they didn't matter at all in the scheme of things. And she mentioned, in no uncertain terms, that only a coward leaves another person to do his dirty work, as I'd left it all to Dario. I should have faced her, like a man.

And, of course, Henri had a few unpleasant things to say about my "little Houdini act." He was angry—I'd hurt Sophie, who hadn't deserved it. I'd abandoned his little girl who needed people to stick around, not to leave her cold. And he reminded me that I'd made a commitment and had bailed. He was disappointed in me, and he was worried about me.

And every one of these people's angry phone messages had ended with a question: "Why are you doing this, to us and to yourself? Why, Philippe?"

Why am I doing this? Why am I making such haste to leave a city that already feels like home? Why am I leaving my niece and my brother who I love like a sister and a father, my new friend and her son, for whom working would bring me the deepest fulfillment? And why am I leaving behind a man who I have come to adore? A man who meets needs that I never even knew I had.

There was a very simple answer; it was really no huge mystery at all. And it could be summed up in one single-syllabled word: fear.

The day before, I'd seen Dario dead on a city street. And maybe he wasn't actually dead—maybe he was actually as alive as ever—but seeing him pale, still, lifeless... it was, very simply, more than I could handle. Seeing him like that reminded me of why I had spent the better part of the last decade hiding.

Love leads to pain. Incomprehensible, intolerable, unsurvivable pain.

I had been through that hell once before when my mother left me. And I might have been only ten years old, but at the very moment I'd come to fully grasp the finality of her death, I had prayed for my own to follow. I'd quickly figured out that there would be no more asking questions and having them patiently answered, no more warmth of being held in loving arms, no more bright laughter to lighten the heaviness of life. My father had not been a man I could relate to on the best of days and who, to this very day, existed on the far fringes of my life. A nonentity in my world, really. Mom had been my single source of light... of life. So the time surrounding her death had been nothing but a visit to hell. I'd lost everything important to me when I'd lost my mother, and that pain had been sufficiently profound that I'd allowed it to shape my entire life from that point on.

And with Dario, I'd broken the single rule that my mother's death had compelled me to establish, through years of personal pain, loneliness, confusion, and anger: *Do not ever love that way again.*

Looked like I'd broken my own Golden Rule, but maybe I had caught myself before I was all the way gone. I hadn't yet moved in with Lauren and let myself become essential to Tommy and her, or them to me. I hadn't fulfilled Sophie and Henri's wishes by completing my role as a loving, dependable family member. And I hadn't moved to a new city to be near my lover so that we could build an "undying love"—a love that I knew very well would someday die.

Because everything died. Everyone did.

So halfway between New York City and Boston, I turned my phone off, stuffed it inside my backpack by my feet, and lay down to catch up on the sleep I'd missed out on the night before.

Alone, as I needed to be.

As I intended to stay for the duration; however long that might be, I hadn't yet decided. I'd think about that later.

26

FOR THE next week, I stayed in a hotel in Medford, Massachusetts, about ten minutes north of Boston. The truth was, I wasn't ready to start on the next phase of my life yet. I wasn't sure what it was going to be… or even *if* it was going to be.

But I knew one thing for sure—my only hope of getting through this was for me to successfully hide from my own emotions. (Not an easy thing to do, but I'd had a lot of practice.) Hand-in-hand with my need to hide from myself was my need to hide from everybody else. I had no desire to see anyone I knew; I'd screwed up royally, and I wasn't even slightly interested in "unscrewing" things. If I went to Henri's house to get my things, well, Henri would be there. And by now, Sophie would be there too. And they'd be angry with me and disappointed as hell, feelings they'd be more than entitled to. Not only that, but my brother and my niece would have plenty of things to say to me that I wouldn't want to hear, despite the fact that they'd all be true.

Or maybe Henri would refuse to even let me in at all. Possibly, he'd have thrown all of my belongings out on the street in front of his house so he wouldn't have to let me in the door… so he wouldn't have to look at me. It would be well within his rights to do so. But I wasn't going to dwell on that possibility either, because it hurt too much.

Like I said, I was fighting hard not to think about anything at all. Which was difficult to do when I spent each day, all day, alone in my Hyatt Place room. At least my room was nice. I guess I'd just stumbled upon a winner in this hotel. Clean, spacious, stylish, had killer peanut-butter-chocolate-chip cookies in a clear glass case in the lobby, not that I had an appetite lately, while not being expensive at all. And I kept as busy as an unemployed family- and friend-abandoning loser-in-love could. I watched movies. I read a couple of bestsellers that I picked up at the CVS down the street, went for walks around Medford Square. Ate pizza and french fries and those amazing peanut butter-chocolate chip cookies on the rare occasions I felt hungry.

You know, I hid—from the world, and from myself. After all, it was what I did best.

And I wasn't a complete asshole, in that I didn't want my family to think that I had died—as of that moment, at least, I was alive and kicking. So three days after I made my break for this big time-out from life in general, I turned on my phone, texted "I'm safe, so go ahead and hate me, but don't worry about me" to Henri, and then turned my phone off again right after the deed was done.

That day, I turned on my phone once more to find that I had twenty-seven voice mail messages. I deleted them all. But before I deleted them, I noticed that nobody had called or texted me for the past three days.

Apparently, all of them were moving on with their lives.

I experienced a fucked-up moment where I felt a surge of relief mixed with a rush of disappointment that I could be so easily forgotten.

And I knew I couldn't stay in this heavenly limbo forever. I also knew that when I finally headed out of my safe hiding spot, back into the real world, I was in for a surplus of pain—the likes of which I'd only felt once before. At that point, it would be time for me to accept the truth of how much I missed him... of how much I'd lost when I'd walked away. It was going to feel a lot like when I'd lost Mom, but this time, *I* had done it on *my* terms. *I* had cut the cord, so to speak, with Dario, and I'd done it the very split second I realized the involuntary loss of him would kill me.

I was destined to feel the pain, since it was starting to look like I was going to press on in life. I couldn't hide from the hurt forever. And I would step out of this temporary respite with that ache already lodged in my heart. I would return to the ocean, where hopefully, I could feel small.

Small enough to get lost among the stars.

But I was gonna hide here for just a few more days.

27

EVER SINCE Mom died, my dreams had been much more about feelings than of specific events. Usually, I experienced layers upon layers of feelings within a single dream; one feeling would peel back, like the outer skin of an onion, just to expose a new raw one underneath. And my feelings dreams usually followed one of several different patterns, that upon waking, I realized was predictable, but when caught in it, seemed so random.

The outside layer of the onion was always a feeling of joy. I could see my mother; she was sort of plump and healthy-looking like before she got sick, and she looked so serene. I could feel her presence beside me too; it was warm and safe. All things good. I was surrounded by that flowery scent of her hair, and she was humming patiently as if she'd been waiting for me. And I was nothing if not elated to be in her company again. I had missed her so much, although I couldn't recall exactly what had happened to keep us apart.

At that point in the dream, I always experienced an intense sense of relief... like I could finally exhale. But somehow a fair measure of apprehension always got introduced the very second after I felt the relief. That's when I always started thanking God for bringing her to me. Over and over, compulsively thanking Him and thanking Him some more, so that He would know that I truly appreciated this wonderful gift of my mother, and He wouldn't take her away from me. This compulsive behavior introduced a seed of anxiety that grew rapidly into a paralyzing fear. And this was when my begging and pleading usually started up... and not to God, but directly to her.

Don't leave me, Mom... I'm not ready for you to go.... I still need you... I'm afraid... please don't go....

And that was always, without fail, when I reached for her... and tried to grab her. To hold onto her so she couldn't leave me. Which was when she began to fall apart into pieces so tiny that I couldn't possibly hold onto them, no matter how hard I tried.

But this night, at the point when I reached out, my mother turned into Dario. And Dario was every bit as elusive as my mother when I tried to grasp him with my greedy fingers. His strong left hand became dust against my palm. So I went for his right hand—the hand that had prepared me for love and brought me to heaven on those few, and memorable, occasions. But with a single brush of my fingers, his hand just melted away. Then with both of my greedy, now-desperate hands, I dove for his face, so I could cling to it tightly and look into those hauntingly beautiful black eyes… but the very second I felt the warmth of his skin between my palms, his face was gone. It burst apart into a flurry of thick black specks of dust that lifted into the breeze, and I knew it would be futile for me to even attempt to catch them.

"Dario!" I shouted into the dark empty hotel room.

Your fear did this to us, Philippe. It was his voice I heard.

I woke up abruptly, knowing that the time had come for me to find out what was going to happen next in my life.

28

WHAT HAPPENED next was that I went back to the ocean. I used my thumbs to get there, which was difficult because I had to travel a lot of distance on the highway. It was easier once I got dropped off at the end of Route 128. From there, in no time at all, I was at Gloucester Harbor.

I spent the entire afternoon down by the harbor asking around about available work on fishing boats, but none of the captains who were docked had any need for another guy. There were a few openings on charter boats, but the work wasn't regular. I'd be more or less filling in when someone was going to be out. And it wasn't what I wanted, anyways. I wanted to be out for days at a time on the endless ocean, with as little human company as possible, not making nice with overeager tourists.

At about seven, I stopped by my friend Bobby's apartment that was located above a restaurant on Main Street. It was as if time had stood still there. I mean, *nothing* had changed. There was a low-key party going on, featuring pretty much the same generic faces as when I'd last been here in the spring.

"Phil—my man—long time, dude!" He grabbed my hand and shook it in his usual funky way, which set me at ease. "Where you been?"

"Shoulder injury, remember?"

"Oh, yeah… I guess I killed *that* brain cell, huh?" He pointed at his beer. "You need a place to crash tonight, man? 'Cause my back bedroom is open, as Gregory the Greek is out on the boat for a few days. At least, I'm pretty sure there will be room back there."

"That'd be perfect. I think I'll take you up on it, bro." I was immediately relieved. Times hadn't changed too much; in fact, it was almost as if I hadn't been gone at all. And despite the fact that I hadn't had any luck finding work today, Bobby Santini was as willing as he'd ever been to let me crash at his hole-in-the-wall apartment.

After Bobby stumbled away, I found my way to the keg and poured myself a brew.

"You back in town, Phil?" It was Bobby's part-time girlfriend, Kathy, who was truly way too cool for a drunk like Bobby, but it wasn't really my place to say so. After tossing her hot pink curls over her shoulders, she reached up and hugged me. "I heard somethin' about you being in New York City. Whu's up with that?"

"I just got back last week." Uh huh, the king of avoidance hadn't lost his touch.

"Yeah, I can see that you're back, Phil, but what were you doin' there to begin with?" Kathy knew how to be persistent. She reminded me a lot of Lauren.

Just thinking about what I had done in New York City hurt like a knife piercing my gut and a bullet to my brain at the same time, which, frightening to say, I didn't think was much of an exaggeration because I was in major emotional pain. An image of Dario and Sophie, their dark and light heads leaning close together as they reviewed a dance sequence, passed through my mind.

"I was checking out colleges with my niece. It was sort of a job for me… for when my shoulder was healing."

"Wow! Really? That must have been a blast. Did you see any good shows or do any of that touristy crap, you know, like visit the Statue of Liberty or go for a carriage ride in Central Park?"

Ouch. Just plain ouch.

"Yeah, I saw the musical *Annie* with my niece, and I actually did have a chance to go on a carriage ride."

"You find yourself a special lady down there?"

Well, that one was easy. "Nah, the only special girl in New York was my niece."

"You're so sweet, honey. Don't worry, I'm sure that special someone will come along for you real soon."

One more time: ouch.

"Anyways, where are you workin' now?"

"I haven't been able to find anything yet, but I just got back."

She stepped right up to me and threw her arm around my shoulders, effectively pulling me down so she could speak into my ear. "You know the restaurant I work at, The Gloucester House, don't you?"

I nodded.

"We need busboys. And desperately."

"Maybe I'll stop by there tomorrow, Kathy. Thanks for the inside info." I figured I'd probably go check it out when I got up in the morning. A job was just a job when you needed the money; I guessed I could survive anything for a while.

I was starting to get tired, or maybe I was again succumbing to my general depression. I had a sudden urge to cuddle up on a big bed with Dario, but since that was never going to happen again, I decided to take my duffel bag into the back bedroom, as I was getting sick of lugging it around. And I was more than ready to say goodbye to another crappy day.

It even hurts to breathe.

When I pushed through Gregory's bedroom door, I was once again struck by how little things there had changed. The bedroom was exactly the same as the last time I'd crashed there in March, the only things missing were the coats tossed all over the bed.

"I remember you."

Having thought I was alone, I jumped backward about a foot at the mental intrusion, and then I looked around to see where the voice was coming from.

"We had a good time together—right there on that very bed. Remember?"

I turned around to see a good-looking blond guy sitting on a chair in the corner. "Uh... sorry." Shrugging, I decided to borrow Bobby's line. "I... uh... must have killed that brain cell." I *really* didn't remember him.

He chuckled, but it was much more of a sneer than a laugh. "Are you kidding, man? You forgot *me*?" He clearly wasn't accustomed to being anyone's ancient history.

I studied him briefly. "Sorry." I took a deep, painful breath, hoping it would give me enough energy to deal with this guy.

"Well, I'm going to have to be extra good *tonight* to make you remember me next time we bump into each other."

I dropped my duffel and kicked it under the bed, knowing that I was not interested in messing around with a stranger. (It looked like some things *had* changed since I was last here.) "Not happening tonight, I don't think." It was barely ten, but I was exhausted... and mentally, down so low. All I wanted was some peace, which could *possibly* come from sleep, if the dreams kept their distance. I pulled off my backpack and shoved it into the side pocket of my duffel beneath the bed, and then pulled off my T-shirt and boots. "Sorry, but I'm gonna crash in this bed *alone* tonight."

The blond guy didn't get up and leave as I'd expected... and as I'd hoped. But that was his problem, I decided.

Although I had no desire to slide between Gregory Panagopoulos's dirty sheets, my energy, both mental and physical, was fast depleting. So I dropped down on top of the bed, without pulling back the covers, since my hygienic standards seemed to be higher than several months before. Then I closed my eyes and waited for the guy to leave, but he didn't move a muscle.

"So, Sleeping Beauty, want some company?" He got up and went to the door.

I opened my eyes, mildly concerned about his attitude, and needing so badly to be alone. "No, thanks." *Good*, I thought, *he's headed for the door*. A cute blond guy like him could easily find his evening's companionship in the crowded party outside the bedroom door.

But instead, I heard a soft click and knew he had locked the door. When I turned over to glare at him, he was pulling off his own shirt. "I'm not too crazy about the word 'no.'"

This can't be good.

Now more alarmed, I fumbled with my own T-shirt, trying to find the neck hole so I could stick it back on.

The guy came right over to the bed and grabbed it from out of my hands. "You're not gonna need that shirt for what I have in mind."

I tried to sit up, but he palmed my throat and pushed me back down onto the bed. I couldn't help but gag. "Leave... me... a-alone...."

His hand remained on my throat. "What if I don't want to? What if I want to leave an impression on you tonight—so you don't go forgetting me again?"

This was not happening. I was not going to get raped in Greg Panagopoulos's back bedroom tonight. I was already slipping quickly into depression—*that* would push me right over the edge.

So with both hands, I tried to pull his hand off my neck, but it wouldn't budge. "Get... off... me!"

He then latched onto my chest with clawed fingers. "I don't think so, caveman! You and me—we're gonna make memories tonight."

And we did make memories, but not the kind he was hoping for. We started wrestling, slid off the bed onto the floor, both of our body weights landing squarely on my bad shoulder, shooting a bolt of angry pain across my back, but the struggle continued on the floor. He was tough and willing to do anything to subdue me, and I was inexperienced at fighting, at best. He scratched my chest, kneed my groin, boxed my jaw, and bit the side of my neck. The second I saw an opportunity to run, I did.

Unfortunately, that meant leaving my shirt, my boots, and my duffel bag behind.

I sprinted through the crowded party, down the stairs, and out onto Main Street. For good measure, I continued my sprint right down to the end of street where I found a place to hide between two cars.

And so there I was—half-naked, barefoot, and I had no spare clothes, personal items, or wallet as they were all in my duffel under the bed in Gregory's room. I just slumped down against the bumper of a beat up Honda Civic and allowed the pain of losing Dario, as well as everybody else I cared for, to make the fact that I was half-naked, homeless, and without a penny to my name seem like a minor inconvenience.

I stayed like that, squatting between a gold Honda Civic and a black Volvo wagon, for a long time.

Between a rock and a hard place, I guess.

And, sure, I felt small.

But there was no getting around it: I also felt stupid.

Because I'd thought I was invisible when I'd fooled around with all of those "nameless" and "faceless" guys in the past. All that time, when I'd thought I'd been hiding so successfully, I was being seen. And remembered.

Since I wasn't one to hold myself to standards like "real men don't cry," I went ahead and did just that. I cried until my tears had washed away some of the emotional numbness I'd been clinging to for the past week.

That's when I admitted to myself that I'd made a mistake. A big mistake.

"I miss them…." I spoke those words aloud. "And I miss *him*."

A few chatty girls walked by my hiding spot, and I stopped rambling and sobbing so they wouldn't notice me. I wasn't yet ready to let the world see me in my desperate half-naked glory.

Once the girls had passed by, I hugged my arms around my chest and added, "I don't want to be invisible anymore, at least not to Dario. I want him to see me so he can love me."

I stood up and patted my back pocket. Thankfully, I still had my cell phone.

"I want to take a risk with Dario… and I want my family back… and I want my friends to trust in me…. I've screwed it all up so badly because I've been so fucking afraid."

Wishing like hell I could rewind time back just over one week, I reached into my back pocket, found my phone, and pressed my brother's contact.

29

"HENRI... HENRI, I'm sorry. I was afraid...." I was crying all over my cell phone, and I didn't even care. "I made a mistake."

"Where are you, Philippe?"

"In Gloucester... I'm in Gloucester. I messed it all up with everybody. I got scared...."

"Philippe, calm down and tell me where you are in Gloucester."

"I thought Dario was dead... and I just didn't think I could do it anymore."

"It's going to be okay, believe me. Now tell me where you are."

"Will you come get me?"

I noticed that he didn't hesitate even slightly. "Of course, I will. That's why I need you to tell me exactly where you are—I'll be there as soon as I get dressed."

"I'm near the corner of Main and Hancock... but Henri, I messed up so badly.... Do you think I can fix it?"

"It's already fixed with *me*, Philippe. Now, hold on.... I'll be there very soon."

TRUE TO his word, Henri was there in fifteen minutes. As soon as I saw his SUV, I darted out from where I was crouched between the two cars. I hurried over to the truck, and when I got in, I folded my arms across my bare chest to cover myself.

"What the hell happened to you? Jesus Christ, you're covered in red marks!" At least his expression looked concerned and not furious. He focused his gaze on my neck. "Is that a human bite mark?"

"I'm fine." I shivered in the AC. "Thanks for coming to get me."

Henri ignored my thank you, but he did reach forward to turn off the air conditioning. "You are *not* fine, Philippe." He looked over at me, and I could see clearly what I'd done to him in the panic-stricken eyes beneath a worry-wrinkled brow.

"I'm really sorry about worrying you. But... but I think... Henri, I really think that maybe there's this part of me that's still only ten years old. It's the part that runs and hides... and doesn't worry too much about anybody but himself."

Henri nodded, accepting that admission. "Maybe you need some help—you know, psychological help—like you did before." Finally, he started to drive.

"Yeah, I think maybe I do." I felt like a kid again. That same messed-up destroyed kid I used to be, but this time, I hadn't watched someone I loved die so there was no good excuse for my behavior.

It was silent for a long while as he drove. Finally, Henri said, "You seemed to be doing so well. I mean, you had an excellent prospect for a job, a future career interest, you'd done so much for Sophie... and then there was Dario."

"I *was* doing well. Henri, I was really happy."

"Exactly what happened in your head when Dario got dragged into the street by that bicyclist?"

That was pretty much the heart of the matter. "I thought he was dead."

Henri glanced over at me, wearing a pained expression. He had been through so much more loss than I had—he'd suffered when his own mother had left our father, and he'd lost my mom, his devoted stepmother, who had passed away when he was a young father, about thirty. He'd tragically lost his wife and son four short years ago—and somehow he was still everybody's rock. I never could understand how he managed it.

"Did it bring you back? To what happened with your mother?"

I nodded. "Thinking I lost him tore me apart, just like losing Mom did. And it made me think of how you lost your wife and son. Nothing lasts, you know?"

Henri pulled into the driveway. "It's almost like you have symptoms of post-traumatic stress from the shock and pain of having experienced so much death, Philippe. But don't worry, we'll figure it out. We'll get you the help you need." He reached across the console and grabbed my hand. "But I can't lose anybody else I love—so *please* never do this kind of thing again." Proud, poised Henri was pleading.

And I knew right then that I wasn't alone in my pain. Henri had more than his own share, and I needed to step up to the plate for him. "I won't."

Baseball analogies meant serious business in our family.

IT WAS the middle of the night, in suburban Essex, Massachusetts, but that didn't stop them all from being there... and forming a straight line across Henri's big kitchen. I was facing a firing squad of eyes; all of them shooting at me with hurt, confused stares.

What are they all doing here?

"I'll get you a shirt." Henri slipped out of the kitchen, leaving me alone with them.

"I'm sorry."

Brilliant intro, Philippe.

I'd never before noticed how remarkably different, in size and color and shape, my loved ones' eyes were. Sophie's pale blue ones were actually rather bright right now. Lauren's large green ones didn't sparkle with fun, as they had the last time I'd seen her but fell upon me with almost a sisterly concern. And Dario's eyes—in those dark eyes I saw everything that I felt in my own heart—hurt, fear, loneliness, and desperation.

Strangely, though, I saw no fury in any of these eyes. But where I needed there to be a measure of understanding, there was only pained confusion.

"Why?" It was just one word, but coming from Sophie, it spoke volumes. She repeated it, "Why?"

Should I dish out the conventional "it's not you, it's me," and leave it at that? No, Sophie deserved more. "I got very upset when I saw Dario... lying in the street... like that. I didn't know how to handle my feelings."

Dario's expression didn't change, but Sophie's softened a bit. "I need you too, you know, Phil. It really hurt me that you left like that."

I felt a tear trickle down from my left eye, only to get lost in my beard. "I was wrong to do that. But I didn't think about what I was doing... I guess I just reacted."

Lauren spoke next. "I wish I hadn't tore you a new one in that phone message, like I did. When we got here, Henri filled us in on what you went through as a boy... and on your depression after losing your mother... and, well, I don't think you're a coward at all, Phil. I'm sorry I said those things."

I studied Lauren carefully. Her soft light-brown hair had been pulled into a high messy ponytail, and she was wearing loose sweatpants with an oversized T-shirt—one of my brother's. I thought that she looked younger and more vulnerable at that moment than I had ever seen her before. "But you were right in that message, Lauren. I *am* a coward. I was running from my fears, and I ended up hurting you and Tommy. *And everybody.*" A few more tears made the trip from my eyes to my beard. "I'm so sorry. I made a huge mistake in taking off like that."

"Don't worry about Tommy; the boy is perfectly fine. He passed out a couple of hours ago on one of Henri's puffy couches after being stuffed full of pizza and ice cream. He just... he just has been asking about why his best friend, Flip... went away... without saying goodbye...." Lauren sobbed once and wiped her eyes.

I shrugged, feeling like such a failure of a friend. Nonetheless, I reminded myself, I was here, trying my best to apologize. That had to count for something, right? Even if they couldn't forgive and forget what I'd done, I could still let them know I was sorry.

Thankfully, at that moment, Henri returned to the kitchen, holding one of my own T-shirts that he must have taken from my storage box in the guestroom. I pulled it on and felt only slightly less exposed, because I knew that everyone here could see the real me: the guy who was now the sheet hanging helplessly on the clothesline, waiting to see what kinds of twists and turns the wind would send its way. And like the sheet in the wind, I waited for Dario to tell me what was on his mind, but he stayed quiet, his piercing gaze never once wavering from my face. I knew that it was my job to make a move toward him, so I forced myself to step over to where he stood, and I took both of his sturdy hands in mine.

"Can you forgive me?"

After a long hesitation, he said, "First, I need to understand what happened."

"Dario, I explained all that to you, about how Philippe doesn't deal well with death. Between our mother dying... and then my wife and son, well, he's seen too much death and he thought you were...." I knew that Henri was trying to defend me, but in truth, I didn't deserve it. I had known that leaving the way I did would hurt Dario, and I had left anyways.

"No, Henri—Dario's right—he needs to understand."

"Why didn't you tell me about losing your mother... and how much it affected you? I do *not* get it, Philippe. Don't you trust me?"

"I *do* trust you—it's *myself* I don't trust, I guess. I just try to keep all of my feelings about my mother inside... like maybe if I let it out, I'll lose control."

"You were wrong—if you keep it all inside, it will eat away at you." I allowed Dario to draw me over to a love seat in the corner of the kitchen. Once we were away from the others, he asked in a hushed voice, "What happened last week? I thought we were happy together." His smooth face was pinched up in all of the wrong places; he wasn't even trying to mask his agitation.

I swallowed hard and then let the truth flow out of me. "I saw you on the street, all pale and still... and I thought you were dead."

Dario nodded and waited for more.

"I felt exactly how I'd felt with *her*... you know, with my mother... at the end."

"And how was that? Tell me, so that I understand."

"Terrified... desperate... alone. I made a split-second decision that I couldn't do it—I couldn't be with you—because I knew at that moment, losing you would tear me apart. So I just shut down my emotions completely."

"I could tell that you were not yourself at all after my accident."

"My heart had already checked out... as soon as I saw your body on the street."

He nodded again, squeezed my hands, and asked gravely, "Did you feel suicidal?"

A very good question.

I shook my head. "That was why I ran—so I could avoid feeling that way."

He studied my expression for a moment, and I was certain that my face betrayed the same level of agitation that I saw on his. "Is this going to be a pattern in our relationship? Every time you get scared, are you going to leave me? Because I love you, and I want you, but I *need* you too, and I cannot go through this again and again."

Our relationship?

He still wanted a relationship after what I'd put him through. "Let me ask you a question." Usually it was Dario asking the questions.

He stared at me, waiting for what I was going to ask him at this critical moment.

"How do you get over fear?"

Dario remained quiet, unsure of exactly what I was asking him.

"What I mean is, how do you deal with loving someone so much that losing him would destroy you?"

I could tell by his tiny smile that he knew exactly what I was asking him now. And he didn't have to consider his answer for very long at all. His reply was at the tip of his tongue. "I guess I just accept that without experiencing fear—without taking that risk with my heart—there is only emptiness. And it is a fair exchange to me."

"Okay," I uttered and then quickly became quiet again as I ran his response through my brain a few times.

As I did so, right before my eyes, Dario shifted back into the confident man I had grown to love. I could see it in the way he pulled his shoulders back, how he lifted his head up, and in the way the severe line of his lips loosened. Mostly, though, it was in the way his dark eyes cleared.

"But I am not the one who can decide if the fear is worth it... to you."

"Will you give me another chance?"

"I will, but only if you are willing to take the risk, and that means you need to come out of hiding... completely. You have to let yourself be as scared as you have ever been. You are going to need to face what you fear most—trusting, loving, and needing me."

"I want to."

He pulled me against him and rasped in my ear, "You are mine. Every part of you belongs to me—and that includes your grief over your mother's death. From now on, you will tell me when you feel afraid." He pressed a firm kiss to my temple. "I know what you need, Philippe."

I nodded against his chest because Dario was already giving me what I needed.

"In a few minutes, I am going to excuse us, we will then go upstairs to the guest bedroom where your things are, and I will show you exactly who you belong to."

I felt one of those scared/excited chills run up my spine. "I'm sorry for what I did."

For a second, no more, he looked at me in such a way that I could see in his eyes how much I'd hurt him, but then his pained expression softened and the poised Dario returned. "I understand that now. But Philippe, I need you too. You are my family... so...."

Still holding his head high, he allowed his eyes to fill, and all I could think of to say was the truth. "I won't leave you again."

AND ONCE again, I was aware that I had never been looked at in precisely that way before.

Dario wore an expression that I couldn't label with a single word, like "hot" or "hungry" or "intense," although it definitely was all of those things. I guess the closest I could come, if I had to label it with a word, would be *possessive*. His dark eyes shone with a sort of craving for me, and I knew for a fact that he was not going to be denied. Dario was going to claim my body, probably with as little trouble as he'd coaxed from me a promise of future honesty. And I was going to let him... and I had a feeling I was going to like it.

I realized I was trembling from head to toe. *With anticipation? With anxiety?* I wasn't exactly sure which.

Bare as the day we were born, Dario made himself comfortable on top of me, surrounding me entirely with his warmth and a sense of safety I needed so much; he stayed there until my trembling stopped. When I was still, he raised his head and shoulders with his strong dancer's forearms so he could look into my eyes.

When our eyes first met, he said with conviction, "You will never hide from me again."

To avoid the intense look of greed I saw in his eyes, I dropped my head down, but he grabbed my beard and used it to move my face back to exactly where he wanted it.

"Look at me, Philippe. Look at who you belong to."

My first response to his words occurred very noticeably between my legs. My dick hardened at the mere concept of belonging to Dario, a man I loved and trusted so much. Though I realized that the way he was talking to me was unusual, many people would probably think it was more than slightly strange, Dario's words of dominance *worked* for me. I had freely consented to the power imbalance in our relationship—nobody had forced me to accept it. And although it was embarrassing to admit, I *liked* Dario's bossy manner with me... maybe I even needed it. I wasn't sure why I had this type of need, but if I had to guess, I'd say it was because Dario's control over me in bed somehow made me feel safe. So I decided I'd look at it this way: the population of Earth was made up of leaders and followers, and it wasn't a crime to like to follow as long as I didn't follow Dario into dangerous or cruel territory. And Dario was an honorable guy, not somebody who would abuse the power he held over me.

It was actually quite simple—my confidence in Dario cleared a path through all of my fear, somehow making way for my own fledgling sense of inner strength.

Tough to grasp, but true.

He spoke in an even voice. "I am going to do whatever I want to you tonight, and you are not going to resist me. If I open your legs, you will keep them open. If I tell you to watch what I'm doing, your eyes will *not* stray. If I ask a question, you will answer me honestly. Do you understand?"

I nodded once, and I nodded again, acknowledging first to him and then to myself that I understood and was willing to do as he asked, despite how far from my comfort zone I found myself. What Dario expected of me was a far cry from being invisible, which was what I was used to. So I rubbed my beard with my palm in an effort to collect myself, and within a minute or so, I came to a decision. I was going to trust Dario, because, at this point, I thought he knew what I needed better than I did, especially in light of my rash actions of the past week.

"Tell me that you understand…right now, Philippe."

I coughed several times, about as nervous as I'd ever been. "I, uh… I understand."

"Good." Dario didn't waste any time; he started his assault on my body with my beard. "I love your beard, Philippe. It is so natural and earthy and uncontrived. But understand this: it cannot hide you from me. I see your face quite clearly right through it." And he took a mouthful of my beard between his lips and drank it in. He sucked on that spot, and then went on to do it to another spot, and another. Soon my beard was soaking wet from his tongue's attention, and I felt as if I'd been washed clean by him.

Dario's next attack was launched on my neck. He found the sensitive spot in the hollow beneath my ear, and he licked and nibbled there so that it both tickled and hurt at once.

"I really am sorry…." The words came out of my mouth on a gasp that was really more of a cross between a giggle and a groan. "I didn't mean to hurt you."

Again, he pushed himself off me and looked straight into my eyes. "But you did." Then Dario's unsmiling mouth descended on my right nipple, and when I just was about to squirm away from his enthusiastic sucking, he mumbled through gritted teeth, "Keep still."

I kept still.

His mouth roved back and forth, from my left nipple to my right, and it seemed like a long time passed, during which I held myself perfectly still, before his lips moved down even lower, and his eyes were level with my groin. I waited for the stimulation I knew he could give me with his mouth, but it didn't come.

When he finally spoke, his voice was raspy and it came forth between heavy breaths. "Take a pillow and put it beneath your head. I want you to watch me love you... and I don't want you to forget what you see."

Obediently, I grabbed a pillow, shoved it beneath my head, and then I watched his perfect lips open and his pink tongue dart out to taste me. I'm sure my gasp was audible to Dario.

"While I am doing this, I want you to explain how you felt when you saw me lying on the street."

"I can't... just... no...." I couldn't say the words, because speaking aloud the words that described my emotions at the sight of Dario's body, still and lifeless on the sidewalk, would surely bring back the pain I wanted to forget. "Please, Dario... I don't want to...."

"Tell me." He dipped his head low and dragged his tongue from the base of my length to the very tip, where it lingered until I allowed another anticipatory gasp.

And then I complied. "I-I... thought you were... dead."

He lifted his lips off me just enough to smirk and say, "But I am very much alive, aren't I?"

I nodded, although he couldn't see it as he'd already returned his fervent attentions to my needy dick.

He was quiet for a while, seemingly intent on giving me a pleasure that I can't even begin to describe, but before I had a chance to fully lie back and enjoy, he mumbled, "Tell me more." Then Dario sucked in a breath and went back to work.

"I felt...." He took me in deeply. "Oh, God, Dario... I felt... like I'd ma-ade a mistake in... in letting myself love you...."

He didn't stop to comment on my confession; he just shook his head back and forth very slightly, pulling my flesh in each direction right along with his mouth. Soon, though, Dario's attention shifted down to my inner thighs. He rotated his mouth back and forth from one leg to the other, up high by my balls, each time pulling a section of my skin between his teeth with a suction so strong that it forced some more secrets from my lips.

"And... and I felt far away... like... like I was on the moon, looking down on y-you and So-Sophie...."

He stopped and looked up at me. "Touch my hair, Philippe. I like it when you touch my hair... and then tell me what you felt when you realized that I was alive."

I needed to use an arm to support my upper body, so I reached down with one shaking hand and let my fingers slide through his silky black hair. When my fingers reached his scalp, Dario started up again, taking me deep. "Uh... uh... oh, God...."

Rather abruptly, Dario released my dick from where he'd held it deep in his throat. "I asked you to tell me how you felt when you realized I was alive?"

This was difficult for me. I felt so exposed. My body, my mind... my heart. I paused. In turn, Dario froze, only returning to his efforts when I again began to speak. "I stopped feeling anything... like... uh... uh...." He slowed down just slightly at my verbal hesitation. "Like at first I was shocked... but th-then I just blocked out... all... of m-my emo-emotions...."

"You completely removed yourself from me, didn't you?" This time, he barely stopped what he was doing long enough to question me. His query just slipped out between brushes of his tongue to my balls.

Nodding, I uttered, "You need to stop, Dario... I'm gonna come... You know?"

He lifted his mouth off me completely, and I shivered. "Yes, I know... and I also know just what you need, Philippe. I want you to repeat what I just said."

"Y-you know... you know what I-I need."

He smiled a bit but didn't return to what he'd been so wrapped up in doing. I wasn't sure whether to be disappointed or relieved. "Look into my eyes."

I did as he asked.

"Now I want to know what you were thinking when you left Sophie and me in that hotel room." Looking up at me, his eyes were bright and maybe a bit wet. I couldn't have looked away, even if I'd wanted to.

This was going to be hard to say, but I'd promised him honesty. "I thought that you'd all be better off without me."

"Did you have plans to kill yourself, Philippe?" His voice broke. A tear slid down his face and landed on the place where my thigh met my groin. "The truth, please."

I shook my head. "I didn't... I really didn't want to die. I just wanted to block out all of my emotions for a while."

Very deliberately, he slithered up my body, and when our eyes were level, he reached over to the bedside table where he'd placed the things we needed to make love. "Did it work? Were you able to block out your feelings for me?" Our chests were pressed together, now slick with our combined perspiration, and he stayed that way for almost a full minute before he finally slid to my side, still waiting for my answer.

"I missed you... but I was in hiding, you know? And I'm pretty good at that."

He shook his head, and I wasn't sure why. "That was your last time in hiding, Philippe."

I nodded one more time, and before I knew it, his lubed-up fingers were working to open my body. I think I might have gasped at the bold intrusion because his entire hand froze for a few seconds, curving gently around my butt cheek, to give me a chance to relax. But as soon as I started breathing evenly again, he got back to it.

Within mere minutes, Dario had shifted me onto my side, and he was on his side behind me, entering me. "Who are you going to go to when you are afraid? Tell me!" His words came out sounding harsh.

I shrunk away from him, but he responded by pushing into me even farther. "Ungh!" I had to blow some air out of my chest before I could manage to speak. "*You*, Dario... I'll go right to you!"

And as he made love to me, Dario continued to inform me in a low rumbling voice *exactly* how it was going to be between us. "In the future, the very moment... the very *instant* you feel the slightest urge to run, you will come to me... and you will tell me about it. And I will listen to you, and I will help you to understand... that we... that we will deal with all of our problems together."

I turned my head in an attempt to get a kiss from him, but he had more to say so he lifted his chin to avoid my mouth. "*I see you*, Philippe. You are not small in my eyes. You are my sun... and my moon... not a tiny star, lost in the heavens."

How did he know that what I'd always wanted most was to blend into the night sky, lost among the stars?

"I see you when you are here with me... and when we are not together physically, I see you in my mind... I *always* see you."

He was getting close to coming, and when he got close, he always gripped my dick in his fist in order to take me there right along with him. He didn't disappoint me.

As soon as I felt his hand on me, I rasped, "Oh... Dario... I'm so close...."

It was as if I hadn't spoken. "You need to face it... right... now.... that losing each other would tear *both* of us apart—but it would be worth the moments we shared together!"

"Yes... yes...."

"Say you love me, Philippe...."

"I love you, Dario...."

"I love you too...." The way he said it made the words sound like a prayer.

As he pledged his love to me, a sentiment only an hour ago I'd feared I'd never hear from him again, I came into Dario's hand, all the while feeling the intimate connection of our joined bodies. The rush of my orgasm took me up to space for a minute, and when I got there, I looked down and clearly saw two young men embracing on an unmade mattress. Then it drove me down, below the surface of the ocean, where even from beneath the water, I could still hear the sounds of Dario's pleasure. And everything was so different from the day Dario got dragged into the street, because this time when I was up high in space, as well as when I was way down below sea level, I was with Dario, not alone.

I could see him clearly; I could hear him perfectly. Dario never left me for a second... and the most surprising part was that I never left him.

"Did you face it, Philippe?"

"Yes... oh, yes... I surely did."

THERE WAS a lot more for me to face tomorrow: Lauren and Tommy, Henri and Sophie. But right then I was being held close to Dario's heart, and I knew, without a doubt, that I was special to him... unique and necessary. And the strangest part of this was that I had no regrets. I *wanted* to stand out in his eyes. And right then, pulled up against his chest with one strong hand, my hair being petted lovingly with the other, I finally relaxed.

"Someone hurt you, Philippe." A gust of warm breath burst into my ear. "I want to know what happened."

"I'm okay now, Dario." I really was. "It was nothing."

But as I should have expected, that answer didn't satisfy Dario. "You need to start listening to me more carefully. I said that I wanted to know… and I *will* know. Because I *need* to know… and to understand… everything about you, Philippe. All of it."

Is he really planning to hold me to this rigid standard of complete honesty?

I swallowed hard. "It's embarrassing."

"I really do not care if it embarrasses you." Another heated exhalation shot into my ear, and I felt my spine stiffen. "I need to know what happened as much as you need to tell me. So go ahead, Philippe."

I looked right past him as I explained; I was humiliated by my weakness, as I hadn't been able to successfully defend myself. "I looked for a job on a fishing boat earlier today. And I had no luck finding one, so I went to this guy I know, Bobby Santini's, apartment to see if I could crash there. Some guy… some guy at Bobby's place tried to mess with me."

Dario's fingers tightened on my back, and he stopped smoothing his other hand through my hair. "What do you mean, 'mess with you'?"

"He wanted us to fool around. He said that he remembered me from before, from back when I was fishing earlier in the year."

"What happened with him tonight, *exactly*?"

This was humiliating, so I closed my mouth, unwilling to continue. But Dario had ways of finding out what he wanted to know. He let go of me and pushed me down onto the bed on my back. As I was still naked, he had no trouble finding each scratch and bruise on my body… and the bite mark.

In his usual persistent manner, Dario pointed to the scratch marks on my chest, and then he ran a finger lightly along each one. "What happened here?"

I still avoided his eyes, but somehow forced out the words. "He tried to beat on me when I said no to sex—he scratched me there." My voice broke, but I experienced a sense of relief that I could share my fear and pain with this man.

Dario seemed angry, and I hoped it wasn't directed toward me because I'd been reluctant to talk. "And here, Philippe? What happened right here?"

"He bit me."

After gritting his teeth, he reminded me in a low voice, "You need to look at me, Phil." Then he lifted his hand to my face and rubbed my bruised cheekbone with his thumb. "And here?"

Strangely, I found it easier to speak when I looked into his eyes. There was a well of strength there, and I could use it... and so I did. "That's where he hit me."

"Did he touch you sexually?"

I shook my head, and then, remembering that Dario liked words, I said, "Other than his knee to my groin, no."

"How did you get away?"

The look of power in his dark eyes sustained my courage. At that moment, I realized that he was lending me the only tool I needed to deal with all of this. I didn't feel nearly as afraid and alone as I had earlier in the night.

"I don't really remember... honestly, Dario. I just remember crouching between two cars on the street... and calling Henri. And that I had to leave my duffel bag at Bobby's. All of my stuff was in it... even my backpack and wallet."

He smiled at me. "Your stuff does not matter. *You* matter. And you got away." Dario leaned down and kissed me, evidently satisfied. "This is how it is going to be, you know. I am going to *always* be asking you questions... and you are *always* going to answer me."

I reached up to pull his mouth back to mine. "I'm okay with that." He kissed me again.

"And no one is ever going to touch your body again but me." He said this so quietly that I wasn't sure if that information was meant for me, or if it was just a sentiment that Dario needed to express aloud. "Thank you for sharing those details with me, Philippe. Tomorrow, we can go to your friend's place and get your bag and your wallet. And we will also discuss in more detail what comes next for us." Dario lay back down beside me, turned, and molded his body to mine. "But now, it is time for us to go to sleep."

30

WE ALL sat around Henri's kitchen table. It was like they were holding some kind of intervention... *for me.* I was thankful for Tommy's presence, as it lightened the heavy atmosphere in the room. He sat on my left side, drawing pictures of a little boy swimming with dolphins, and singing softly, "There's a hole in the bottom of the sea." On my right was Dario, who hadn't left my side since last night when he'd led me to the love seat to talk privately. A few minutes before, he had pushed our chairs together, and now his hand covered mine, where it rested on the table.

And I couldn't help but notice that Lauren sat as close to my brother as I sat to Dario. I had a feeling that something was going on between them, and I was glad.

"So what comes next for you, Philippe?" Henri liked to get right down to business as much as Dario did.

"I... I just wish this never happened. I liked how everything was going before." That was an honest admission. "I was happy."

Lauren leaned forward. "Then I vote that we move forward as if it didn't happen. I believe that everyone is entitled to a mistake."

"Would you still let me take care of Tommy?"

Tommy, hearing his name, looked up and smiled. "Hi, you guys."

We all laughed, but I was waiting with a big lump in my throat for Lauren's answer. She looked at me directly. "Nothing has changed as far as I'm concerned. Phil, you are the best person in New York City to look after Tommy."

I glanced over at Dario. He squeezed my hand and smiled and then nodded toward Lauren, as if I should give her an answer.

"I'd really like to take care of Tommy."

"Then it's settled. Phil, this was merely a bump in the road for us. And believe me, there will be more bumps. Sometimes I will cause the bumps, sometimes it will be Tommy, and other times it will be you again. But we'll figure out how to get past each of them."

I thought right then that maybe I loved her too. "Okay, Lauren."

"And you'll live in our spare room?"

"If you still want me to."

"*I* do! I want you to live with me, Flip!" Tommy piped up. "What 'bout that other thing you guys was sayin' before… you know, 'bout Dori?" He was so cute—he called us Flip and Dori—like we were Disney characters.

"How would you feel about having a roommate?" Dario asked me this quietly. "And there is no correct answer to that question. I want you to tell me honestly if you feel ready for me to be your roommate at this point."

"You mean, you could live with me at Lauren's?" I looked around and saw that Lauren and Tommy were both nodding.

"Yeah, Phil. I think we'd all benefit from the feeling of family we'd get from living together… if you feel comfortable with it, of course."

"Okay… uh, th-that would be great." Despite my stuttering, I meant it. Dario squeezed my hand again. "I feel strong when you guys are around me. And maybe I won't need your constant support forever, but I really need it at this point."

"We all need support, Phil. We'll be there for each other." Lauren smiled, satisfied.

Then Sophie plopped her elbows on the table, loud enough for all of us to turn in her direction. "Phil, I've been wondering something…. Like, well, was the summer good for you? 'Cause it was *so* good for me—and I'm not talking about just the dancing, but also about *us*. I thought that you and me were like best friends, you know?"

"Flip is already *my* best friend," Tommy interjected, looking worried.

"Best friend who is a *girl*, then," Sophie corrected herself with a wink to the little boy.

I got up out of my chair and went over to stand behind Sophie's chair. Then I leaned over and hugged her around her neck. "I really do think we are friends, Soph, and yeah, we really did get close. Honestly, you were part of the reason I took off. I was worried that I was starting to care for you way too much, but Dario's going to help me to deal with those feelings."

"Can I come and visit you this fall?"

I looked over to Lauren for her approval. She nodded. "You bet, Sophie. Whenever you want… our door is always open to you."

"And Lauren and Tommy might be coming here to visit us this fall, as well. We have a plan to go apple picking, right, Tommy?"

Tommy replied by saying, "And we're gonna make apple muffins, Hen-ree. You said so…."

We all looked over at Henri. "Philippe, your friendship with Lauren and Tommy has brought two very special people into our lives. In fact, Lauren and I have planned an upcoming weekend together, so I'll be visiting the city with Sophie within a week or two."

Lauren looked at Henri, and then at me. "I have big plans for your brother, Philippe. Maybe you, Dario, and Sophie could watch Tommy one night so I can take Henri out on the town."

"Of course. That sounds great." I smiled, but it fell right off my face when I noticed Henri's expression, which was still quite troubled.

"But in all seriousness, Philippe, as your older brother, I'd like to keep taking care of your health insurance until you have a job that provides benefits. And with the insurance provided, I'd really be pleased if you looked into getting some counseling." Every once in a while, Henri looked uncomfortable with a particular demand, and this was one of those times.

But I put his mind at ease. "I think you're right about that, Henri. And thank you for continuing my health insurance." Once I was settled in my new apartment and had figured out Lauren's work schedule, one of my top priorities would be to find a counselor so I could finally deal with the impact my mother's death had on my life. So that maybe when I remembered her, it could be with joy, and not just pain.

Having expressed their concerns and seeming to be satisfied with my responses, the faces around the table appeared much more at peace than they had last night. My family and friends believed me when I said that I'd finally come out of hiding, and they somehow trusted that I could stay out, for my own sake, as well as theirs. And I was going to give it my best effort; I couldn't continue to pull Houdini acts whenever I felt threatened.

FOR A long time, I'd thought that I'd mastered the art of hiding. At first, I accomplished this by blending into the vastness of the night sky over the ocean and more recently, into the chaos of a busy city. But I'd been mistaken. I knew now that I had always been visible, despite my best efforts to hide. The only one who had been fooled into thinking I'd been invisible had been me. It seemed that I had been trying to hide myself—my worries, my fears, my pain—inside myself.

Which just plain didn't work.

And as of right then, I was finished with it.

Thanks to the ones who surrounded me, those who saw me clearly when I didn't want to be seen at all, I had been flushed out of hiding.

Epilogue

"YOU ARE going to nail your audition today—mark my words." Dario was completely confident, which provided Sophie with what was necessary to boost to her confidence. "So no worries, okay, Sophie?"

She trotted up to us and gave us each a big hug and a kiss. "Okay… well, wish me luck."

"You do not need luck to get into SUNY Purchase; it is practically a done deal." Dario sniffed once and then shifted his attention to Tommy. "Would you care for a game of Hungry Hippos, Tom?"

As Tommy scrambled to the toy box to find the game, I stepped over to the door where Henri, Lauren, and Sophie were pulling on their coats. "Once they see you dance, Soph, you'll be golden."

"Thanks for that, Philippe." She smiled up at me, her pale blue eyes sparkling with anticipation, like maybe she was looking forward to her dance audition, rather than dreading it. "I feel pretty good about what I'm going to do today. And you know how much I love the solo. I'm ready for this."

"And if they don't let you in, I'll donate a building to the school—that should do the trick to change their minds." Henri might have been chuckling, but I knew that he was still semi-serious.

Lauren and Sophie caught gazes and rolled their eyes at the same time. "Sophie will do just fine without the construction of the Henri Bergeron Dance Theater on SUNY's campus." She tucked a stray wisp of Sophie's blonde hair into her tight bun. "Come on, honey, we don't want to be late." Then she opened the door, and the girls headed for the elevator.

Henri shrugged and looked over at me. "See you guys afterward. And I'm thinking we'll eat in the East Village tonight, sound good?" He stopped and appeared to be consumed in deep thought for a moment. "But let me check it out with Lauren before we call it an official plan."

I nodded and watched him leave, confident that Sophie would ace the audition. She'd gained so much poise since we spent last summer here together. She was more confident in terms of her dance abilities, as well as more relaxed in her attitudes toward her own body. And Sophie was dying to return to live in or even near the city that had become her second home.

"Lauren has become quite motherly toward Sophie, wouldn't you agree?" Dario asked from his spot on the floor where he pounded incessantly on the green hippo's lever, trying to trap as many colorful marbles as possible before Tommy's quick-moving blue hippo scarfed them all up.

"Yeah. She's been good for Sophie—finally, the girl has a female influence in her life. And I'm pretty sure she knows how to keep Henri in line too." I had to smile at the thought of Henri, and how lately he'd been struggling to think before he spoke, and how he was always sure to run his big ideas past Lauren before declaring them to be the law of the land.

I dropped down onto the carpet beside Tommy. "Looks like Tommy's blue hippo is hungrier than your green one, Dario." Tommy smirked at Dario victoriously. "But the yellow hippo just told me that he is hungrier than the green and blue hippos put together."

"Are you gonna be the yellow one, Flip?"

"You bet I am! So watch out!" The three of us proceeded to challenge each other to at least fifteen games of Hungry Hippos, until Tommy informed us that his thumb was starting to get numb.

"Well, I know that these hippos have had plenty to eat, but how about a snack for my two favorite guys?"

Tommy nodded at me as he grabbed the remote, snapping on the Disney Channel. Before Dario followed me into the kitchen, I heard Tommy say, "Make sure he puts in peanut butter, 'kay, Dori?"

"Consider it done, Tom."

When Dario got into the kitchen, he leaned on the small table and winked at me once. "So what is it going to be today—peanut butter and jelly, peanut butter and fluff, or peanut butter and honey?" I simply couldn't get Tommy to eat any sandwiches without peanut butter in them. Not that it was a bad thing.

"How about if I surprise you?" I opened up the breadbox and took out the whole wheat bread, and then I grabbed the peanut butter and jelly *and* the honey from the cupboard, thinking that this would be a new twist on the PB&J. But before I'd gotten anything done in the direction of making sandwiches, Dario had molded himself snugly up against my body and was groping me. "You seem very hungry, Mister Pereira."

"No, I just love the way you make a PB&J. In fact, I cannot resist it...."

Dario loved being part of a family. He thrived on all of the simple traditions that we shared—telling each other how our days went, celebrating birthdays with candles stuck into cupcakes and noisy off-key singing, tucking Tommy, and each other, into bed every night—right down to eating as many meals together as possible.

"Hey, I forgot to tell you with all of the excitement of Sophie and Henri coming into town, I got an A minus on my Basic Ideas in Math test. And the professor read part of my paper aloud in Freshman Composition."

He turned me around and pushed my backside against the granite countertop. "That's my good little Einstein."

"I like the math class better, though, because it is more related to the education program."

"It looks like you have found your niche." Dario's cool hands had slipped up beneath my T-shirt, and his fingers were soon tracing my abs and moving north. "What is the grin for?"

"Because it looks like *you've* found my nipples.... Are you sure PB&J is what you're hungry for right now?"

Dario turned me back around, but not before I'd looked deeply into his warm dark eyes. "For your information, there is a nonsleeping child in the house. So I suppose I will have to wait until tonight when I have you all to myself in the privacy of our bedroom, to satisfy my *other* appetite. But I want you to keep this in mind: if you thought those Hippos were hungry a little while ago, you have not seen anything! I am going to devour you...."

I got one of those chills up my spine. Not exactly a new sensation anymore, but still, it managed to make me think. And I was torn as to whether I should respond to his words with, "promises, promises" or "I can hardly wait," so instead, I just drooled a little bit.

Dario stepped back, and I could feel his eyes on me as I whipped up our sandwiches. "Don't you think that all of us have done a good job of building one complete family, where there were just fragments of different families last summer?"

I looked back over my shoulder, thinking that his question had come from out of left field. I realized that Dario cherished our newly formed family, but I had no idea where he was going with his statement.

Still, I nodded and agreed. "We sure did."

"I am so glad that you let me in. Know what I am getting at?"

I waited for more. It was kind of a role reversal for us; usually, it was Dario waiting for me to explain things.

"You opening up to all of us—that was the seed that made this family grow."

I cut each sandwich in half and then turned around to look squarely at my lover.

"If you had kept on hiding yourself, Philippe, Lauren would be alone here with Tommy, and Henri would be alone in Massachusetts with Sophie… and you'd be somewhere on the Atlantic."

He was probably right about all of those things. But there was more to it than that…. If I hadn't opened up my heart, I wouldn't have reached the point I was now at, where I could think about the wonderful mother I had and smile. It had taken hard work, plenty of counseling sessions and a willingness to trust in my family and friends, and in Dario. But I slept soundly now, those awful nightmares usually kept their distance.

Dario's eyes filled, just a bit. "And I wouldn't have you… and this family."

I stepped forward, pulled Dario's smooth face against my furry one, and whispered into his ear, "I have nothing to hide anymore."

"That's what I like to hear." He held my head in place and planted wet kisses on me, first on one hairy cheek and then on the other.

"Hiding always sounded so good until I couldn't find a safe spot to hide anymore." I took a single step back so that I could see Dario's face, but he refused to release my cheeks from his grasp. So I changed tactics and whispered into his ear, "And maybe it took me a while, but I learned my lesson. Nothing good comes from hiding among the stars. I'd rather be out here in the sun with you."

MIA KERICK is the mother of four exceptional children—all named after saints—and five nonpedigreed cats—all named after the next best thing to saints, Boston Red Sox players. Her husband of twenty years has been told by many that he has the patience of Job, but don't ask Mia about that, as it is a sensitive subject.

Mia focuses her stories on the emotional growth of troubled men and their relationships, and she believes that sex has a place in a love story, but not until it is firmly established as a love story. As a teen, Mia filled spiral-bound notebooks with romantic tales of tortured heroes (most of whom happened to strongly resemble lead vocalists of 1980s big-hair bands) and stuffed them under her mattress for safekeeping. She is thankful to Dreamspinner Press for providing her with an alternate place to stash her stories.

Mia is proud of her involvement with the Human Rights Campaign and cheers for each and every victory made in the name of marital equality. Her only major regret: never having taken typing or computer class in school, destining her to a life consumed with two-fingered pecking and constant prayer to the Gods of Technology.

Contact Mia at miakerick@gmail.com.

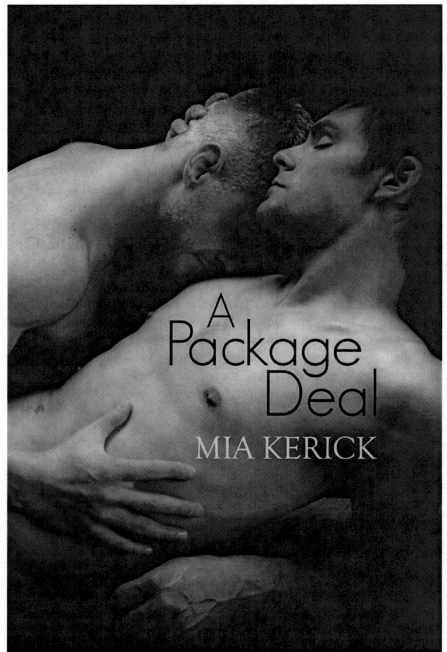

Also from MIA KERICK

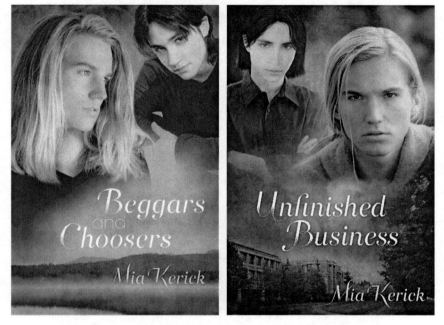

http://www.dreamspinnerpress.com

CPSIA information can be obtained at www.ICGtesting.com
Printed in the USA
LVOW12s0629260714

396136LV00003B/220/P